Clues & CHILLS

BOOKS BY
JANET RAYE STEVENS

The Beryl Blue Adventures in Time

Beryl Blue, Time Cop
It's Been A Long, Long Time
Every Time We Say Goodbye
The Suitcase: A Beryl Blue Time Travel Short

Time Travel Suspense

The Titanic Time Heist

WWII Paranormal Suspense

A Moment After Dark

Romantic Suspense with a Supernatural Twist

The Fateful Knight

Mystery & Suspense

Clues & Chills:
New England Stories of Mystery & Murder

Contemporary Holiday Romance

Cole for Christmas

Clues & CHILLS

New England Stories of Mystery & Murder

JANET RAYE

AWARD-WINNING AUTHOR

STEVENS

GREAT BROOK PUBLISHING

Printed in the United States of America. First printing, 2024

www.janetrayestevens.com

ISBN: 979-8-9901207-4-7 (print)

979-8-9901207-5-4 (digital)

For my friend and writing pal Sharon Healy-Yang,
who loves a mystery
—and a good cup of tea—as much as I do.

Take a road trip through New England with these sometimes dark, sometimes funny, but always gripping tales of mystery and murder. From a roadside diner in Boston to a 1950s movie theater to murder on the Maine coast and beyond, this collection of clues and chills will keep you guessing until the last page.

Contents

DIRTY WATER   1

MURDER AT THE BIJOU THEATER   15

MRS. FEATHERPATCH COOKS UP A MURDER   47

MRS. FEATHERPATCH & THE CASE OF THE SKEWERED HAM   81

ECHOES   111

MURDER AT MIDNIGHT   139

THE HOT SEAT   169

BERYL BLUE: TIME COP sneak peek   185

Chapter One   187

About the Author   198

DIRTY WATER

Massachusetts

Our journey through New England starts here, the home of the American Revolution, the Boston Red Sox—and some shady characters gathered at a Boston greasy-spoon diner.

"What'll it be today, hon?"

The waitress tipped the coffee pot and filled my cup. Young, too young to be calling an old fart like me *hon*. She wore one of those diner waitress uniforms, an orange polyester dress that clung to her smooth, long-legged body. She was almost a carbon copy of Lucille, except her eyes, a washed out blue. Lucille had eyes the color of violets, like Liz Taylor.

I studied the menu board hung above the rectangular window pass-through to the kitchen. There were a couple of Vegan meals listed but not much else had changed since I was last here in September 1967. When the Red Sox were on their way to the World Series, my best pal Shorty Quinn was on his way to Vietnam, and I was a two-bit thug of twenty-five on my way to nowhere.

The waitress tapped a long fingernail painted with sparkles and stars onto her order pad, telling me I better decide fast what I wanted to eat. I chose the pot roast dinner, the same meal I had eaten that night long ago.

The waitress swung her hips away and I spun my stool to give the old place a once over. Back in '67, this place was a seedy dive. Now it was retro chic, a classic lunch car diner with lots of chrome.

The smudged windows looked out at a pot-holed parking lot and the piece of Route 1A that tore through Revere on its way up the Massachusetts coast. Booths with vinyl-covered seats lined up across the wide aisle from the Formica counter that ran almost the entire length of the joint. The only thing missing were the jukeboxes that once sat at the end of each table and at intervals along the counter.

I turned back to my coffee and waited for my meal. It had been more than fifty years since that love song to Boston, "Dirty Water," played on those jukeboxes. Fifty years since the first and only time I came here. Fifty years since I looked into Lucille's hopeless, violet eyes and knew what I had to do.

Fifty years since the night I killed Eddie Philbin.

I slid onto a stool and slapped my hat and the late edition of *The Boston Globe* on the counter. Frankie Valli's latest hit "Can't Take My Eyes Off of You" warbled out of the jukebox speakers. The diner was stuffy, warm, and busy for so late in the evening. Guys in suits like me, gals in skirts down to the knees. No love beads or hippies at the Beachside Diner. It catered to a different kind of crowd.

"What'll it be, hon?" the waitress asked, filling my cup with coffee.

She smelled of lavender perfume and dish soap. Food and coffee stains covered her apron and splattered her orange dress. Lucille, her name tag declared. She looked tired, but man was she a beauty. Sweet, with a bow mouth and apple cheeks, like a kewpie doll I won at a Revere Beach arcade when I was a kid. Silky blonde hair, long legs, lots of curves, and eyes the color of violets in spring. I ordered the pot roast dinner and pretended not to watch her hips swing as she sashayed away.

The song "Light My Fire" came out of the jukebox next and I went back to minding my own business.

I stirred a lump of sugar into my coffee, added a splash of cream, and sipped while I scanned the *Globe's* front page. There was the usual politics and weather, but the rest of the stories were all BoSox glory and Carl Yastrzemski's slamming bat as the hometown team raced toward the pennant.

A commotion broke out at the door. I looked over my shoulder to see Eddie Philbin push inside, followed by a couple of rat-faced goons with muscled arms. I knew Eddie. Everyone in Boston knew that small-time hood. He liked to think he was Mr. Big Stuff, but he was just a punk. He and his buddies flopped into a booth and Lucille hustled over there with coffee. Eddie's hand found her ass and stayed there the whole time she filled their cups. Lucille barely flinched. His hand had been there before.

One of the goons fed a quarter into the jukebox at their table and punched in some numbers. "Dirty Water" started to play. Eddie sang along. A tall, slender fella, he favored sharp suits, like Sinatra in one of his Rat Pack movies. Eddie was no Sinatra.

He slapped Lucille's fanny and sent her on her way, turning his attention to his coffee and his two pals.

I watched Lucille move around the diner, tending to her customers. The regulars. She joked with them, asked about the family, listened to them bitch about their crappy jobs.

"Don't be getting any ideas about her, Mac," the guy two stools down said. He had beady eyes and a beak for a nose. "Lucille is Eddie's girl."

She might be Eddie's girl, but she didn't like it, that was for damn sure. There was no light in her eyes when she looked at him. More like fear.

"That's a shame." I sipped my coffee. It wasn't the worst cup of joe I'd ever tasted. Not the best either. "What's she doing with a punk like that?"

Beak Nose shrugged. "What's any girl doing with any guy? Poor thing's got a couple of kids and a husband dead in Vietnam, what else she gonna do? She can't survive on measly tips. Needs someone to take care of her."

"The way of the world, I guess," I said, going back to my newspaper. Hiding my anger. The way of the world ate up and spit out girls like Lucille. Chewed

7

up guys like me too. People desperate for cash, desperate enough to do anything to get it.

A while later, a plate slid across the counter under my nose. Piled high with pot roast and potatoes, steaming hot and smothered in gravy. There was a spot of green there too. Spinach, maybe.

"Here you go, hon," Lucille said.

I looked up from my newspaper into her pretty face. She was the All-American girl, except for the bruise under one eye. Covered with makeup, but not quite. She didn't even try to hide the bruises on her arm and around her wrist.

"Thanks, doll." I eyeballed her nametag again. The blocky letters had been punched out on one of those label-making machines and stuck to a piece of plastic. "Lucille. Nice name. My mother's name was Lucille."

It wasn't, but Mother was a Lucille in a lot of ways. Stuck in an empty life. Taking a man's fists. Lying about the bruises and broken bones. Walked into a door or tripped on the rug, she would say. No one believed her excuses, but no one said anything. No one did anything either. Except me. I stopped my father's fists for good, the first stop of many on my road to sure damnation.

Lucille fiddled with the chain of a silver locket hung around her neck, eyeing me. "I've never seen you here before. What brings you to a dead-end greasy spoon like this?"

Though tempted to glance at Eddie, I dipped my gaze to my plate. "I heard the pot roast was good."

She topped off my coffee, flashing a soft smile. "Well, mister, you heard wrong."

That coaxed a grin out of me and a laugh from her that cut off as "Dirty Water" came around again on the jukebox.

"I'm not fond of this song," I said, picking up my fork, watching her. "Give me Johnny Cash or something else with some hurt in it."

"It's Eddie's favorite song." Her voice dropped low. "He thinks it's about him."

"Lucille!" Eddie barked and the whole diner went still.

She closed her eyes in a weary way. Her hand wrapped around the locket at her throat. There were pictures of her kids in there, I guessed, maybe the dead husband. I wondered how long it took for Eddie to swoop in after her old man bought it in Vietnam.

My gaze followed her as she gripped the coffee pot and dragged over to Eddie as if meeting her executioner.

"You're gonna get your thumbs broke if you're not careful," Beak Nose warned. He sounded like he was eager to watch, should it happen.

I told him to go pound sand and dug into my meal. Lucille was right. The pot roast was lousy, but the potatoes were edible, and the gravy was wet. I ate slowly and when I'd finished, I nursed my coffee and took my sweet time reading every word in the *Globe*, including the ads and stock quotes. Lucille took care of her customers but avoided me. She kept Eddie's coffee cup full.

"Dirty Water" played again, then "Ode to Billie Joe" and "To Sir, With Love" managed to muscle their way onto the jukebox. Eddie wolfed down a burger and slurped who knew how much coffee. Soon, he stood and headed to the can. He passed Lucille clearing a table and grabbed her, his fingers digging into her shoulders. He kissed her neck. She tossed him a fake smile that faded as soon as he disappeared down a narrow corridor around the corner.

I waited a few seconds and followed Eddie. I stopped at the cigarette machine at the corner and lingered, like I couldn't decide if Winston tastes good or if I wanted to get the honest taste of a Lucky Strike. Outside, a spanking new Mercury Cougar roared up Route 1A, snagging the attention of Eddie's goons.

That's when I made my move.

The door was closed but not locked. Good. Easier for me to slip inside. The bathroom was no more than a box with a toilet and a sink. And Eddie, taking a piss. He jerked toward me, but I moved fast and had him on his knees, head in the toilet before he could yell for help.

Eddie put up a fight. He was strong. I was stronger. I'd worked hard to make sure of it. "Dirty Water" piped up again. The music wailed over the speakers in the diner, drowning out the sounds of Eddie's struggles and water splashing. He balled his fists and flailed wildly, trying to punch me, but I held him down tight. His thrashing slowed, then stopped. His fingers uncurled as his body sagged, going still.

I straightened and caught my breath, then washed my hands, dabbing at the wet spots on my sleeves with a paper towel. I fixed my tie and looked down at that punk who thought he was Mr. Big Stuff. Who believed the way to a girl's heart was through his fists.

"How do you like that dirty water now?" I muttered.

I left Eddie with his head in the toilet and made my way back to my seat at the counter. I had to scram before the goons missed their pal and went looking for him. Even their pea brains could put two and two together.

I dropped two bucks on the counter for my meal and tucked five hundred-dollar bills under my plate for Lucille. The money she'd paid me for this job.

This one I did for free.

I put on my hat and left as "Dirty Water" faded away on the jukebox.

The waitress with the sparkly fingernails brought me my meal. The pot roast wasn't much better than it was fifty years ago, but the gravy was wet, so I dug in. I pored over the *Boston Globe* on my phone as I ate. Conversation rose and fell around me. The music was soft, piped in from one of those satellite radio stations. I didn't recognize the songs.

I'd traveled a long road since that night in '67. I'd done a little time, but not for Eddie. The cops never caught up to me for that. To tell the truth, I doubted they looked too hard for that punk's killer. I got nabbed on a robbery gone wrong and sent to Walpole for twenty-to-life. The way of the world. I'd fought the law, and the law won. For a while anyway. I ratted out a couple of shady characters I used to run with and managed to get an early release.

I'd straightened out somewhat after that. Lived what I wouldn't call a good life, but it was a life. Some regrets. Not about Eddie, though. That was my one, true act of redemption in a lifetime of sin.

Didn't save my soul. I was bound for the hot place no matter what. But I hoped what I'd done had given Lucille a chance to live a better life.

A woman's hand pushed a piece of paper under my nose. My bill. She'd scrawled *Paid* across it in large, purple letters. I squinted, confused.

"Compliments of one of our regulars." The waitress nodded toward a trim woman seated in a window booth.

The woman was pushing eighty but still looked like a million bucks—silky, snow-white hair probably styled at a pricey Copley Square salon, a tailored suit she'd no doubt picked up at an exclusive shop on Newbury Street. The only thing downtown about her was the vintage silver locket that hung around her neck.

She met my gaze and lifted her coffee cup in a silent toast. I returned her soft smile.

She had violet eyes.

MURDER AT THE
<u>BIJOU THEATER</u>

New Hampshire

Moving north up Route 1 and traveling seventy years back in time, we visit the Granite State, where we buy a ticket to a movie theater in 1951. *The Day the Earth Stood Still* is playing on the big screen, but murder is the theater's main attraction.

LILLIAN SWEPT SPILLED POPCORN into the dustpan with an old broom that had seen better days. Greasy butter sopped into the lobby's threadbare carpet, joining a thousand other stains dating back to 1920 when her father and grandfather opened the Bijou Theater in their hometown of Manchester, New Hampshire. That was a week before Lillian was born. She'd grown up with the place, and though now only thirty-one, she'd grown old in some ways too.

Grandpa was gone now, so was Pop, her mother, and Lillian's husband, killed at Iwo Jima. And now she feared she was about to lose the last thing she loved.

The Bijou.

Lillian dumped the popcorn into the waste bin near one of the exits. She remembered the crowds that used to swarm the ticket booth and throng the lobby, buzzing with excitement as they pushed through the doors into the theater itself. In the old days on a Saturday night, the place would be mobbed. Tonight, a whopping eight people sat in a theater of two hundred seats. Ten people, if she counted the twin boys of about seven who'd darted ahead of their harried-looking mother into the building.

Lillian could blame the fine late-September weather for so few tickets sold. Or the drive-in theaters that seemed to have sprung up in every suburb like crabgrass. But she knew the truth. Television had upended her world, keeping customers at home with their eyes glued to that miniature monster's sixteen-inch screen.

She doubted the Bijou's rival theater uptown, the Rialto, had experienced such dismal ticket sales. They had a big Hollywood premiere this weekend, *Showboat*. Lillian looked across the lobby, to the poster of their current feature film, *The Day the Earth Stood Still*. A huge robot clutched a scantily clad woman in its arms while Army tanks fired at the metal beast willy-nilly. The folks who'd ventured away from their television sets to go to the movies tonight probably preferred *Ol' Man River* and Ava Gardner in Technicolor over this odd, black-and-white science-fiction picture.

Lillian wedged the broom and dustpan into the corner next to the popcorn-maker as Bernie, her concessions man, scuttled across the lobby, gripping a comic book.

"Well, you sure took your time," she said. Bernie had stepped away from his post behind the counter to use the washroom what seemed like ages ago.

"Sorry, Lil," he said, not sounding sorry at all. "Had some tummy trouble. But the feature's already started, who's gonna pop out for Milk Duds now?"

She scowled. "Someone might. One more candy sale might help us break even this week. Help *you* keep your job. I suggest you do your reading on your own time."

He slapped his comic book—*Batman*, she saw—on the shelf under the counter with the rest of his stack, muttering something about lady bosses Lillian didn't care to ask him to repeat. She left and circled the lobby again, looking for more things to tidy up.

She shouldn't ride Bernie. She'd already lost three concessions men to that new factory manufacturing home appliances that had opened on the outskirts of the city. Bernie would be the fourth to hand in his notice if she kept nagging him. But she couldn't have him slacking on the job. Grandpa and Pop would never have let him get away with lollygagging.

And neither would she.

Lillian stopped at one of the entrance doors leading into the theater. She ran her hand over the swinging door's worn padding and looked through the window, as she'd done since she was a child and grew tall enough to peep through the glass. As always, a thrill tickled her belly when she peered inside.

On the screen, a giant metal man stood like a menacing sentry in front of a flying saucer. The tinny sound of the actors' voices and music reverberated from the speakers. Carpeted aisles ran along both sides of the theater, with the seats clustered in the middle. Light from the projector flickered over the customers' heads. Far fewer heads than in the Bijou's 1930s heyday, when films like *Gone With the Wind* had played to a packed house for weeks and weeks.

Lillian saw the familiar sequence of three dots flare at the edge of the film, warning the projectionist that the reel was at its end and to switch on the second projector. That would make the transition between reels seamless. It didn't happen. The picture faded and a space of white—the tail of the film's first reel—followed. Someone in the audience yelled up to the projection booth. Seconds later, the second reel began.

She frowned. Herman had been the Bijou's projectionist for twenty years, except the two years when he was in the army during the war. He'd *never* missed his cue. Not once. Was he getting careless, like Bernie? Or discouraged, counting the days until they closed and he had to find another job.

A silhouetted figure seated in one of the front rows caught her eye. Slumped to the side, most likely asleep. That happened. A *lot*. The customer had paid for their ticket, they could nap through the movie if they wanted to. But sleepers also sometimes disturbed the other patrons with their snoring. She'd better wake him up before he could bother anyone.

She eased the door open. The smell of popcorn and cigarette smoke rolled out. She crept down the aisle and reached the front row in no time, finding a man slumped down, with his head against the back of the seat. He'd dropped his drink cup and popcorn container. Orange-colored soda pop puddled around his feet and popcorn speckled the floor.

"Sir," Lillian whispered, getting no response. She looked around the theater. None of the other customers seemed to notice her or the sleeping man. She grasped his shoulder, giving it a shake.

The theater brightened as the movie's scene changed from night to day. Light reflected on the man's face. Lillian stifled a cry. He wasn't sleeping. Not by a long shot.

His eyes gaped wide open. Unseeing.

Dead.

Lillian had to read the police department's number in the telephone book three times before it made any sense. Her hands shook so much as she dialed, her fingers kept slipping out of the number holes. Panic threatened to overwhelm her. And so did worry, as a host of selfish thoughts gripped her. What would this do for business? Who would want to come to the Bijou now, where customers died in their seats?

She knew she had to call the police, but she also hoped she could keep the man's death quiet.

A curt voice answered. Lillian asked for Detective Chet Diamond, hoping he was on duty tonight. She'd grown up with Chet. He'd been her brother's childhood friend, a few years older than her, always around their house. And the Bijou. She hadn't seen him since he went to war, but she knew he'd joined the police force when he came home. Chet had always been calm and capable, and that's what she needed now to help her figure out what to do.

She was in luck. Chet picked up the phone with a brusque hello. Hearing his voice after all these years comforted her.

"Chet, its Lillian Thornton. I mean Lillian Dow, from back on Hanover Street. Do you remember me?"

An uncomfortably long pause followed. "Of course I do. Little Lillian, who pestered me and your brother Dennis without mercy when we were kids. What can I do for you?"

She took no offense to his teasing. She'd been as pesky as a mayfly back then, always flittering around. She blushed even now to remember what a crush she'd had on Chet.

"I'm sorry to bother you, but..." She took a steadying breath. "I'm at the Bijou. We have a slight problem and I need advice on how to handle it."

"Problem?" He sounded suspicious and official at the same time. Perhaps it hadn't been such a good idea to call him.

"You see, uh, one of our patrons has, well, he's expired."

Another long pause. "Expired? You mean he's dead?"

She sighed. "Yes, that's what I mean. I'm not sure what to do. Should I call the coroner?"

"Leave it to me. I'll be there in ten minutes. No, make that eight."

Eight minutes to the second later, Chet strode through the lobby door. Tall, broad-shouldered, not as slim as he had once been but as handsome as ever, with those light brown eyes and sandy blond hair. No gray at all. Not true in Lillian's case. Silver shoots had taken up residence in her auburn curls like unwelcome guests.

Chet shook her hand with a firm, comforting grasp. "Lillian. It's been too long. Sorry to see you again at such a time, though." He released her hand but held her gaze. He cleared his throat. "I heard about your husband. I'm sorry."

"Thank you." She gave him a tight smile, grateful he didn't go into detail or ask questions. She didn't have any answers to give. She'd received a telegram reporting Doug missing in action at Iwo Jima, presumed killed, leaving her staring into a gaping hole where her life used to be.

"How's Sylvia?" she asked. Chet had married Sylvia Davis shortly after she and Doug had tied the knot.

His expression turned brittle. "That didn't work out."

Lillian murmured her regrets but wasn't surprised. He'd married a woman he barely knew, only a few days before he shipped out. An impulse, her brother Dennis had said. A hurry-up marriage that wouldn't last, Pop had said. Pop had seen too many of those in the first world war.

Chet drew himself up as if putting all that behind him. "All right, Lil. Where's the dead man?"

She led him across the lobby. He opened the door into the theater and waved for her to step inside ahead of him.

"I haven't been here in a long time," he said. He sounded wistful.

"You're not the only one. Attendance has been way down. Well, matinees have been good, but the evening shows—"

"Shh," a heavy-set man in the last row hissed.

Lillian and Chet moved down the aisle side-by-side. On the movie screen, the film's stars were trapped in a stopped elevator after the electricity had blinked out across the city. Chet reached the front row first and squatted next to the dead man's seat. He pressed two fingers to the man's throat, checking for a pulse, then looked over the body intently. Lillian stood next to Chet and watched, both curious and horrified by his gruesome examination.

"I think I see what killed the poor bastard," Chet said softly, glancing up at Lillian.

"Was it his heart?"

"In a manner of speaking."

He flipped the man's suit jacket open, revealing a small knife—stuck into the dead man's chest.

"Right to the heart," Chet said, sounding impressed. "Not a lot of blood. He died almost instantly."

"You...you mean... Murder?" Here in the Bijou? In her home.

Chet gave a terse nod and bile rose in Lillian's throat. Cold raced through her veins. Pins and needles prickled her scalp. She feared she would faint, as she had that awful day she'd gotten the telegram about her husband.

"Hey." Chet stood and gripped her by the shoulders, his eyes firm on hers, warm and reassuring. "We'll have none of that. This is serious, Lil. I need your help. You need your wits about you. Can you do that?"

She nodded, unable to speak.

"Good." He released her, peeled off his suit jacket and draped it over the dead man's face. He turned to her. "I want you to stop the film and gather everyone in the lobby."

Lillian scanned her customers scattered around the theater—two men, one heavy, one thin, seated separately in the last row, a woman fairly close by, her hair tied up in a scarf like *Rosie the Riveter*, a skinny youngster at the opposite end of the front row, an older couple behind him. And up above, next to the projection booth, the young mother and her twins, watching in the privacy of the darkened quiet room.

Lillian looked back at Chet, finally finding her voice. "Do you think one of my customers is responsible?" she asked in disbelief.

He answered with a grim smile. "That's what I mean to find out."

———

Chet had called in a report to his station house by the time Lillian had assembled everyone in the lobby. The customers milled about, creating quite a hubbub for such a small group—the people who'd been seated in the theater, the mother and her towheaded twins, Herman the projectionist, and Bernie, who put aside his comic books and reluctantly joined the gathering.

Lillian watched Chet place the contents of the dead man's wallet onto the concession stand counter. Her mind raced, still unable to comprehend what had happened, barely able to think the word, *murder.*

"The man's name is John Sanderson," Chet said, studying an identification card. "Lives over in Portsmouth. Kind of a hike to come here just to see a movie. He was a veteran, served in the war."

"Who didn't?" Herman said then asked, "What's going on? Why did I have to stop the film?"

Chet ignored him and continued to go through the items taken from Sanderson's wallet. A matchbook from Howard Johnson's, a few dollar bills, some loose change, and a coupon for ten cents off the Bijou's evening show.

"I've been sending those coupons out," Lillian said, her cheeks warming with embarrassment. "Trying to drum up business since Uncle Miltie and his television gang started stealing our customers."

Chet nodded, and did she detect a slight smile at her weak joke? He'd always been kind to her, even when she'd tagged along after him and her brother when they went fishing at the Merrimack River. Even when she refused to go home when Dennis told her to scat.

"How long are you going to keep us here, Mister?" the young mother, a pretty blonde, asked. "I've got to get my boys home. It's already past their bedtime."

Her children barely seemed tired the way they chased each other around her legs and tumbled across the carpet, but she looked exhausted.

"What's your name, Ma'am?" Chet asked. "I didn't see you in the theater."

"It's Gladys Smith," she said, sounding so unsure Lillian wondered if the name could be an alias. "I was watching the movie in the quiet room with my boys."

Chet raised an eyebrow. "Quiet room?"

"A private room for families," Lillian said. "I added the room last year, hoping to compete with the drive-ins. Converted Pop's office next to the projection booth upstairs, where he used to keep the gin during Prohibition. I asked Herman to install speakers and had some workmen cut through the wall and put in a window to watch the movie through."

"Clever," Chet said.

"I would hardly call it a *quiet* room." Mrs. Smith shot a woeful look at her rambunctious boys. "More like a place to put all the noise and not bother anyone else."

"I see your point." Chet chuckled. "Well, Mrs. Smith, you'll be able to leave as soon as I get some answers." He scanned everyone assembled, studying each of them closely for a moment. He held up Sanderson's identification card with a picture of a dark-haired man with worried eyes. "I'm Detective Chet Diamond, and I want to discover why and how this man was murdered. Here, tonight."

Cries of shock and disbelief rippled through the group. Lillian's shoulders seemed to droop all the way to the floor.

"Surely you don't think any of *us* had something to do with it," the heavy-set man who'd shushed her and Chet earlier called out.

"Maybe, maybe not." Chet placed the dead man's identification card back on the counter with his other belongings and turned back to the group. "My guess is Mr. Sanderson was killed shortly after the film began. He sat in the front row, to the left. I want each of you to tell me if you spoke to the man, if you left your seat during the movie, or if you saw anyone else get up." He shifted to the heavy-set man. "I'll start with you."

The man claimed to have been glued to his seat from the minute he entered the theater until

Herman had stopped the film and turned up the house lights. Chet questioned the thin man who'd also been in the back row, and he claimed the same.

Chet turned to Lillian next. "Lil, were you in the lobby the whole time? Did you see anyone leave? Notice anything unusual?"

"Yes. I mean no." She couldn't believe how nervous his questions made her. His piercing gaze had her wanting to confess to every crime under the sun. "I was outside in the box office selling tickets until shortly before the newsreel began. I came into the lobby after I closed the ticket booth. Once everyone entered the theater, I didn't see anyone come or go. Except Bernie. He stepped away from his post to visit the facilities. He was gone a long time."

Chet swung toward Bernie, who leaned causally against the counter.

"As I told Lil, I was indisposed." Bernie pressed a hand to his midsection.

Lillian nodded in confirmation and Chet asked, "Did you see anyone in your travels, Bernie?"

"Nope. Not a soul."

Chet's attention swiveled back to Lillian. "What about earlier, before the movie started? Did you see the dead man? Speak to him?"

"No. I only spoke to him when I sold him a ticket."

Chet turned to Herman. "You're the projectionist, right? You have a full view of the theater. Did you see anyone speaking to the man, or coming near him?"

"No, no one."

"You could've turned your back and missed seeing the culprit." Lillian stiffened. "Or you could've left the projection booth. You missed the cue to change film reels. That's something you never do. What happened?"

Herman's expression turned squirrelly. "Oh, yeah. I guess I looked away. I was... I was boxing up the newsreel to send back to the distributer." He abruptly changed the subject. "I saw the dead fella *before* the film. In the lobby. I saw him with *you*." He gestured to the woman with the *Rosie the Riveter* headscarf. "You were both in line to buy popcorn. You were talking."

Bernie jumped in. "They weren't talking, they were arguing."

The woman's cheeks paled but she eyed Chet with a defiant look. "I *was* arguing with him. He was behind me in line and got mighty fresh. As a nurse, I'm constantly put upon by mashers who think it their right to pinch my fanny or whisper something crude in my ear." She lifted her chin. "I told him *exactly* what I thought of him."

"Good for you," Lillian said. She'd had her share of run-ins with men like that. "Did you speak to Mr. Sanderson again?" She cut off. "Oh, sorry, Chet. Didn't mean to step on your toes."

His lips twitched. "No, do carry on, Detective Thornton."

Wise guy. She turned back to the nurse. "I noticed you were seated closest to the dead man. Did you see anyone near him during the movie?"

The woman took a moment, as if scrambling for words. "I don't think so. I'm afraid I snoozed through the incident and most of the picture. I worked a double shift today and I'm completely worn out."

Chet's eyebrows shot up. "Why come to the Bijou if you were tired? Why not go home?"

She sighed. "I wish I could. You see, I live at home with my parents. You know that radio program, *The Battling Bickersons*? My folks make them look like a loving couple. I came here to catch forty winks in peace." She squinted, as if trying to see something far away. "Now that I think of it... I might've been dreaming, but I thought I saw someone moving about in front of me."

All eyes followed the nurse's gaze as it drifted to a tall, skinny kid of about seventeen wearing dungarees and a short-sleeved plaid shirt. Lillian had noticed the young man earlier, sitting at the opposite end of the row from the dead man.

"What're you looking at me for?" the kid squeaked.

Chet studied him. "Aren't you George Winthrop? Officer Winthrop's kid brother? You work at Lou's filling station over on Elm." George gave a reluctant nod. "You usually work on Saturday nights. What're you doing here?"

"I...I..." George swallowed convulsively, his Adam's apple bobbing in a furious cha-cha. "All right, I confess. I called in sick to work. I wanted to see this movie in the worst way." He shot Chet a pleading look. "You won't tell Lou, will you? He'll fire me for sure."

Chet's eyebrows rose again. "Don't worry, your secret's safe with me. As long as you answer my questions. Did you get up during the movie? Did you speak to Sanderson?"

"No. I was in my seat the whole time. I never spoke to him at all."

"That's not true," the heavy-set man piped up. "I saw you talking to him in the lobby."

Chet crossed his arms and tapped his foot, scowling at George. "Out with it, son. What really happened?"

George hung his head. "Okay, I spoke to him. He was in a hurry to get to the concessions counter and bashed into me. I lost half my popcorn. I called the fella a clumsy jerk and that's it."

Chet eyed Lillian again and she nodded. She hadn't witnessed the encounter, but that explained the spilled popcorn she'd swept off the carpet.

"I never saw the guy, or went near him after that," George added, then stabbed a finger at Bernie. "But *he* did. He talked to him a long time."

Bernie flushed with anger. "Yeah, I talked to him, you dunce. He gave me his order for popcorn and a drink. He paid, I told him to enjoy the show, and I swear, that was it, Detective."

George snorted, clearly unconvinced, but Chet moved on. He turned from the teenager and Bernie to the older couple, a balding man and a petite woman in a severe purple suit.

"What about you, Mr. and Mrs....?"

"Morton," the man said. "The wife and I mind our own business, so naturally we didn't see a thing."

"Not quite, Sam," Mrs. Morton said, sounding sheepish. "At one point I bent to straighten the seam in my stocking and happened to glance over my shoulder." She eyed Mrs. Smith. "I could swear I saw *you* slip out the door of that room up above."

Mrs. Smith let out a nervous laugh. "You must be mistaken. I never budged from the quiet room until we were asked to come down to the lobby."

"No, Mommy." One of the twins, the one missing his two front teeth, tugged on her skirt. "You did leave. You said you had to go pee-pees."

"Billy, that's not true." She shooed the boy away.

"It *is* true. You said you had to go, and you were gone a long time and Bobby ate all my popcorn."

"Did not," Bobby cried.

"Did too," Billy countered and chased his brother around the concession counter like Tom and Jerry in the cartoons.

Now all eyes fell on Mrs. Smith. She let out another nervous giggle. "I suppose I *did* leave for a teeny second. But I didn't go near Mr. Sanders, or whatever his name is...or, uh, was."

"Then where did you go?" Lillian asked. "I saw no one near the powder room after the film started."

Mrs. Smith flashed a panicky look at Herman. He tugged at his collar.

"*Oh*," Lillian said, the truth dawning. *That* was why Herman had missed his cue to change the film reels.

"I get it." Bernie let out a blat of coarse laughter. "I wonder what Mr. Smith thinks about you sneaking away to canoodle with the projectionist in the dark."

Mrs. Smith's face went beet red. "It's not like that. My husband walked out on us two years ago. Simply disappeared, the louse. I've been struggling to raise my boys alone. Herman's the first decent man I've met. He's kind to me, kind to my boys, too. So, you can put your judgmental thoughts in your back pocket, mister, because I am having *none* of them."

Herman smiled and lifted Mrs. Smith's hand to his lips. "In fact, I've asked Gladys to marry me." His eyes brimmed with happiness. "And she's agreed to make me the happiest of men."

Lillian's heart lifted at such a joyful outcome. Chet wasn't as touched.

"Felicitations," he said, mighty grouchy. "But we still have a mystery to solve. Who killed Mr. Sanderson and why?"

"It wasn't me or my wife." Mr. Morton glared at Herman and his newly minted fiancée. "Maybe the lovebirds did it together."

Mrs. Smith huffed in indignation and Herman spat, "You're out of your mind."

"What about her?" The thin man swung toward the nurse. "She sat close to the dead fella. Could've killed him with no one seeing."

"And a nurse would know exactly where to stab a man," Bernie put in.

"That's a lie," the nurse cried. "I had no reason to kill him. I didn't even know him."

"How do we know *you* didn't do it?" The heavy-set man jabbed a finger into Lillian's face.

She vehemently shook her head as everyone erupted into shouts, accusations, and finger pointing worse than an unruly session of Congressman Joe McCarthy's Communist-hunting committee.

"Quiet!" Chet shouted, like the stern and commanding platoon sergeant he used to be. The whole mob instantly shut up. "Let me get this straight. No one saw anything. Everyone saw someone." His gaze touched on George, the nurse, and Bernie. "And the three of you had a dust-up with the man."

Lillian gasped as something Bernie had said earlier flashed into her mind. Something that had given him away. "Bernie, how did you know Mr. Sanderson was stabbed? Detective Diamond never mentioned it."

"You're right, Lil." Chet whistled. "I'll be damned."

Bernie's eye popped and he sputtered a denial.

"Mommy, look what I found." One of the twins raced out from behind the concessions counter. "It's dirty. It's got syrup on it."

He held up a *Batman* comic book—smeared with blood.

His mother shrieked and tried to snatch it away, but the boy clutched it to his chest. "It's mine. Finders keepers."

Chet squatted next to the boy and tousled his hair. "Here, son, let me have a look."

"Okay." The boy handed it to Chet. "It's a Batman comic. I like him."

Chet examined it, then stood and raised an eyebrow at Lillian. "Blood. I bet if we test the knife handle, we'll find traces of ink."

Bernie edged toward the door, but Chet grabbed him by the collar. "Don't even think about it. I want your explanation, and fast."

Bernie squared his chin and faced Chet. "Sanderson was in my platoon. One night I made a mistake. I wasn't paying attention and some fellas got killed. It was an accident." His words poured out in a dull monotone. "Sanderson didn't see it that way, though. He tracked me down. Asked if we could meet. We had a drink at the Howard Johnson's between the matinee and tonight's show. I told him to bug off. Told him the past can't be changed no matter how much we want it to. I left, thinking we'd settled the whole thing."

He shifted position and balled his fists.

"Then Sanderson showed up here. He threatened me. Said he'd report me to any of the Army brass who'd listen and tell the families of the men killed what I'd done. I told him to go sit down, watch the movie, and we'd talk afterward. I knew I had to stop him. I took a knife from my lunchbox, the one I use to cut apples, and slipped into the theater when Lil wasn't looking. Then I..." His voice turned flat, emotionless. "Bayonet training came in handy."

Chet went as still as a corpse. Except his eyes. They glittered, piercing Bernie to the bone. "You hid the knife in the comic book. You folded it around the knife to keep your fingerprints off the handle. And then you stabbed that man in cold blood."

Bernie nodded. "I did. And you know what? I'd do it again."

———

Chet stood by Lillian's side as the police escorted the handcuffed Bernie out of the theater. Men from the coroner's office followed, rolling the stretcher bearing Sanderson's sheet-covered body through the front door.

"Poor Mr. Sanderson." Lillian dabbed her eyes with a handkerchief. "And Bernie. To be so lost he'd do such a thing. What a tragedy."

"I know, Lil." Chet's voice was gruff. "For some people, the war never got over."

She sighed and looked toward the customers still in the lobby, waiting for their turn to talk with the police. Gladys Smith sat on a bench with her sons nestled against her. The twin dynamos had run out of steam and were fast asleep. Herman stood close to her, hovering attentively. The heavy-set man and the nurse were deep in conversation. George Winthrop paced back and forth, practically wearing a hole in the carpet.

"I know you're worried about what this all means for the Bijou," Chet said, following her gaze. "In my experience, people are drawn to the sensational. I bet these folks will be back tomorrow. I bet you'll have a packed house every show the next couple weeks."

She brightened. A little. "And then?"

"I don't know. We'll figure something out."

Her heart fluttered to hear that plural pronoun.

Chet gave her an odd smile. "You know, Bernie had one thing right. We can't change the past. We can only look to the future." He scanned the poster advertising *The Day the Earth Stood Still*. "This looks like a fun picture. Maybe I'll stop by for the matinee tomorrow. It's my day off. Will you be here?"

"I'm here every day, Chet."

"Good. I'd like to see you some time when there's not a dead body involved."

She laughed, feeling young and new again. And hopeful, for the first time in a long time. "I'd like that, Chet. If you don't think I'd pester you too much."

He grinned. "I'm thinking you can pester me all you like, Lil."

"Pardon me?" George said. He'd crept up to them while Lillian had been gazing into Chet's eyes. "Do you think you could put the movie back on? I'm anxious to see how it turns out."

MRS. FEATHERPATCH

COOKS UP A MURDER

Maine

It's only fitting we get two stories while visiting New England's largest state. Join sassy sleuth Mrs. Featherpatch for a double dose of mystery, mirth, and murder.

First up, the actress who plays the beloved TV sleuth Mrs. Featherpatch discovers a gruff small town police chief and a real life mystery are the perfect solution to chasing away her troubles.

A WHITE-HOT FLASH FROM a camera burst to life across the street as I came up off the beach, lighting up the side of my hotel. Oh, hell. *Paparazzi.*

How'd those jackals find me? I'd fled here to coastal Maine, off season, and registered at a quaint, out-of-the-way inn under my real name to get away from them. And all the other buzzards wanting to feed on my pain. My fresh pain. My husband Jack had left me dozens of times during our thirty years together, his thirty years as king of the box office. He'd always come crawling back. I'd always forgiven him. But this time was different.

This time, I'd left him.

Another camera flash. Okay, make that just *one* paparazzi skulking in front of the building, but still... Here I was, the meticulous Antoinette Picasso, Toni to my friends, dressed down in sweats, no makeup, gray roots on glorious display, and my face probably as red as a cooked lobster from my morning power walk along the beach.

I dragged a sleeve across my drippy forehead and took a cleansing breath. Surely I could slip by and into the hotel with a brisk "no comment" before that shutterbug could pounce. Pasting on my best Hollywood premiere smile, I crossed the street. *Ready for my close-up, Mr. DeMille.*

The camera flashed one more time, igniting a *duh* moment. That was no paparazzi waiting for me. The uniform should've clued me in—she was a police officer on the job. As were the other cops on the scene, gathered around something on the sidewalk.

A chill shivered over me. The *something* they clustered around was a body. Here I was, thinking it was all about me when it was some poor... What? Male or female? Hard to tell from the pile of clothing accordianed onto the pavement.

The police picked up on my presence and swiveled to gape at me.

"Hey, it's Mrs. Featherpatch," one cop, a woman, blurted, blinking in recognition.

"Whoa, Mrs. Featherpatch," her male counterpart echoed.

The photographer's camera clicked wildly as she went paparazzi for real.

Le sigh. There had been a time when few people recognized me outside of my TV character's gray hair and makeup. I was still young when I took on the role of seventy-something Delphinia Featherpatch. Okay, maybe not *young* by Hollywood's standards, but I'd barely hit fifty when I donned the sensible shoes, floral prints, and blue hair rinse of that delightfully sly character.

"Listen, sweetheart, it's a one-off movie of the week," my agent Rocco had said at the time. "Grandmotherly TV chef stumbles on a murder no one else can solve. Think Julia Child meets Jessica Fletcher. Good money, too, doll."

Not just good money, great money. And with roles for actresses my age that didn't involve playing a clueless mom or wearing judge's robes dwindling, I took it. The show killed in the ratings. America fell in love with *Mrs. Featherpatch Cooks Up a Murder* and a multi-year acting gig was born.

Flash forward a dozen years and I'd reached a point where I didn't need as much aging makeup or padding around my butt to fill sweet old Delphinia's grandma jeans.

Or to be recognized by fans.

"It's me, guilty as charged," I said. "Don't let me disturb you, officers. I'm just going in." A lie. I was going nowhere. I couldn't tear my baby blues away from the body. "Uh, what happened?"

"Guy fell out a window," said female cop, whose nametag read Marie Johnson.

Well, that was blunt. "Poor thing. Do you know who he is?"

"Guy."

"No, I mean, do you know his name?"

"It's Guy." Male cop this time. His badge read Donnie Dash. "Guy Hurt."

I winced. An appropriate name, considering.

"He fell from the eighth floor, we think."

I followed Donnie's gaze up the side of the brick building, the facade scored by years of New England weather and sea air. Another cop poked his head out the open window far above.

"We'll find out more when the chief gets here," Donnie said. "Unless you have a theory, Mrs. Feather...uh, Ms. Picasso?"

Seriously? "Officer, I'm not a detective, I just play one on TV—" Something caught my eye. Guy plummeted eight stories. He must've pounded the pavement when he landed. His skull was cracked. Why so little blood? "Are you sure he fell?"

Donnie pursed his lips. "Think he was pushed?"

"Not exactly. Perhaps he was thrown. As in, already dead and someone pitched him out the window." At least, that's how it happened in episode #03-01 of my show, *The Case of the Flour Child*. "See, there's not much blood. Wouldn't there be more if his heart was still beating when he hit the ground?"

The cops lit up, as if that was the most brilliant deduction ever. Donnie and Marie leapt on Guy and flipped him over. There, sticking out of his chest was a small knife.

Aha. And, huh? I was right?

"You cooked up the answer," Donnie said, quoting the tagline from my show. The only thing missing was the cheesy end theme music swelling and a freeze frame of my face.

"The answer to what, Donnie?"

A man as tall as a redwood, dressed in running gear, trotted up. The crew of cops swung toward him.

"The case, Chief. Mrs. Featherpatch said Guy was already dead, and damn if she isn't right."

The chief and I entered a sort of mutual inspection society—I sized him up, he gave me the once over. I had no clue what he thought of me, but he passed my inspection with flying colors, what with the muscles his snug Colby College sweatshirt and running pants hinted at underneath, his dark hair shot through with silver, and his rugged, lived-in face, like he'd been out at sea for a decade. *Hot*. AARP side of sixty hot.

Down girl. I'd come here to get away from men. At least, one man in particular. My husband—now *ex*-husband—and his baggage that I'd let drag me down for thirty years. To nurse my wounds and take a little Toni time. Not to ogle the local beefcake.

"You a cop?" he asked. Quite brusquely, I might add.

I lifted an eyebrow. "No."

"Medical Examiner? Amateur embalmer?"

Both eyebrows up now. Those questions offered a two-for-one special, brusque *and* snide. If it weren't for his adorable Maine accent, I'd be annoyed. "No on all counts, Chief."

"Then, Mrs. Featherstone, if you don't mind..." He gestured toward the hotel door.

"It's Mrs. Feather*patch*. I mean, it's not really, I'm Toni—"

"I don't care who you are. You don't work for me, so beat it."

Well. I don't know what disturbed me more, that he dismissed me so rudely or that he had no idea who I was. How could he not? *Mrs. Featherpatch Cooks Up a Murder* had been on broadcast TV and streaming for years. Even the young cops recognized me, and they weren't even close to my show's demographics.

"All right, I'm going, Chief Pushy McTyrant. But you should know I *didn't* find the answer. Look at the knife wound. No blood. Unless that knife acted like a stopper in a bottle, wouldn't there be blood if he was stabbed to death?"

"Gosh chief, she's right again," Marie said.

The chief winced, maybe made all kinds of other irritated faces, but I didn't stick around to find out. Antoinette Picasso knew when to make an exit.

———

Showered, I put on my makeup, donned a silky blouse, casual-elegant wide legged jeans, and a cashmere cardigan, then called down to the kitchen for breakfast. A few minutes later, a commotion in the hallway got me to the door. If it was my food, it'd be the first time in the history of room service that an order was delivered in a timely fashion and still warm.

But nope, not my lobster omelet, just the town's finest swarming over dead guy Guy's room down the hall. Trying to put the strange pieces together. I mean, dead when he went out the window, maybe dead when someone plunged a knife into his heart. How'd he die, then? Who stabbed him then defenestrated him?

The police chief chose that moment to step out into the hallway. He strode toward me, glowering. *So* hot.

"You see anyone up here today or last night, Mrs. Featherbottom?" he asked with all the politeness of a bear rousted from hibernation.

"I'm not Mrs. F— Oh, whatever. Yes, I did. Last night, I saw a woman go into his room around eleven."

He straightened. Goodness he was tall. "You remember what she looked like?"

"Not really. It was late. I was a tad...sleepy."

"Sleepy, eh?" Chief McMuscles accused.

"Okay, I was a bit tipsy." A lot tipsy, actually, leaning toward pickled. I'd polished off almost a whole bottle of some delicious local vintage with a lobster on the label in the hotel bar. "I was celebrating."

"Celebrating, eh?"

Scintillating conversationalist, this one. "Yes, celebrating. Just got sprung from a thirty-year sentence." Funny to think of my marriage and its bitter end that way, but there it was. Not what he wanted to know, though, so I dug into my brain, trying to cut through last night's Shiraz haze. "When I came up from the restaurant and got off the elevator, I saw a woman duck into Mr. Hurt's room. Medium height and build, dark hair that covered her face, unfortunately, so I couldn't get a good look. Dressed all in black and..." I paused for courage. "Large breasts."

A corner of his mouth twitched, but he managed not to go all dopey over the B-word. My now ex would've been panting like one of Pavlov's dogs.

"You sure of those details?" he said. "You said you were...sleepy."

He'd abandoned snide and moved directly to sarcastic. "Yes, Chief. I'm positive. Now I have some questions for you. What'd you find in the room? If the fall and the knife didn't kill him, what did? Any idea who tossed him out the window?"

"That's still to be determined." Police speak for *mind your own business*. He gazed at me intently, as if he suddenly realized he'd seen my photo on a wanted poster on the post office wall. "You know, it's possible you were the last person to see Guy Hurt alive."

"What's that supposed to mean? You seriously don't think *I* had anything to do with the poor man's death." Yikes. Did I just deliver that clunky line? *The* most clichéd line in all detective fiction, usually uttered by the guilty party as they scrambled for an alibi.

"I can't say. We haven't had a murder in our little village in twenty-five years. You come along and now I have a dead man on my hands."

He was joking. I hoped. And seriously, that was a plot right out of my TV show. In fact, a storyline recycled at least once a season when Mrs. Featherpatch just happened to be in the wrong place at the right time and found herself accused of murder and in desperate need of digging herself out. Full disclosure, I hated those episodes. They were tedious and required a tremendous amount of suspension of disbelief.

Yet, here we were.

I batted my eyelashes. "And what, exactly, would be my motive for blowing into town and taking out a man I never knew existed until only a few moments ago?"

He shrugged, surely a taxing chore, what with those broad shoulders and all those muscles. "To irritate me?"

"Chief, while I would take great pleasure in irritating you, let me assure you, if *I* were going to commit a murder, you would never find the body. Or me. Case closed."

"Sounds like you've given this some thought."

I narrowed my eyes. "I'm thinking about it right now. Especially if you keep up with such ludicrous accusations."

He scowled. Magnificently. "Relax, Mrs. Feathertwig. I doubt you came here just to knock off one of our finest citizens." A bell dinged and he glanced down the hall to where a contingent from the State Police spilled off the elevator. "But in case I'm wrong, I'll need you to stay put." He paused, a hint of mischief in his eyes. "You could be our number one suspect."

I did not stay put.

If I balked at doing what Jack told me to, rarely did what the director on set asked me, and no longer did what that bastard of an agent wanted after he got me strapped for eternity to Mrs. Featherpatch, how could that autocratic Andy Griffith think I'd listen to *him*?

I went shopping. Spent the morning prowling the shops that were open this early in the season, snapping up souvenirs, and asking questions. About Guy Hurt's life, who he pissed on, and who he pissed off. I hadn't been wearing Mrs. Featherpatch's inquisitive cardigans all those years for nothing.

"Everyone knows he liked the ladies stacked," a saleswoman in a quaint little pottery shop said when I asked about Guy's late night visitor. "And he played around. A lot. One woman after the other." She wrapped the kiln-fired lobster paperweight I'd just bought in tissue paper. "It's a good thing Guy didn't have a wife at home pining for him while he tomcatted around."

She broke off, looking uncomfortable. A wife like me. Sitting at home, waiting for Jack. Forgiving him.

For too many years I was like the wronged wife in episode #07-11, *Meringue and Murder*, standing by her man. Convinced he wouldn't stray again, convinced *this* time we'd put it back together.

Plain truth, I stayed because I was in love with him. Not Jack Dane, movie star, but Chester Arkwright, the funny but needy and often insecure guy I fell for when we met as extras on that Schwarzenegger flick in the '80s. I'd hung on for the right reason, our kids, and for the wrong reason, my pride. But no more. The kids were grown and on their own. And we were done. For real.

After the saleswoman *have a nice day*-ed me out the door, I zipped my new windbreaker with a lobster logo on the front and strolled back to the inn. The Guy puzzle was beginning to take shape, but many pieces were still missing.

"Uncork me a bottle of that lobster-y Shiraz, Pierre," I said to the burly man with thinning hair behind the bar as I took a seat. "And a bowl of lobster stew for lunch." I loved lobster, Jack didn't. I was determined to stuff myself with the shellfish every chance I got from now on.

As I waited, I sipped my wine and scanned the restaurant, done up in warm tones, with ship's lanterns and lobster traps dotting the walls, and huge picture windows offering a view of the cove. Busy today, with most tables occupied. Glasses and silverware clinked, conversation buzzed, and wait staff fluttered about. A busboy who could be a twin of Norman Bates from *Psycho* cleared a table, looking furtive, as busboys often do.

I tried to remember the players who'd been dining and drinking here last night. Had the well-endowed woman I'd seen going into Guy's room been one of them? Was she present now? No woman fit the bill.

The bartender plopped a huge crock of stew under my nose. Steam wafted up, giving me a lobster and cream facial. I took a blissful taste of heaven on earth.

"Have you heard about Guy Hurt?" I asked Pierre.

"Of course." He topped off my wine. "Nothing happens in town I don't hear about."

"Tell me what you know. And none of that customer-bartender confidentiality stuff. Tell me what you told the police."

Maybe my straightforward approach loosened his lips, or more likely the fact I was a good tipper, because, as I ate, he blabbed like a gossip columnist. Most of what I'd already heard. Guy wasn't exactly a model citizen.

"Pierre, you ever see Guy with a brunette, medium build, large rack?"

Oh, the smirk! Men and boobs—doesn't matter how big or small, perky or not, those things brought out a guy's inner moron. Even my old girls, getting better acquainted with my bellybutton by the minute as they sagged south, often got the once-over.

"Chief already asked me that. The only girl I ever saw Guy with was Wendy."

He tipped his head toward a woman helping another waitress clear a table. Wendy had the right cup size—especially compared to her companion—but she was blonde and taller than the woman I scraped from my Shiraz-hazed memory.

I tapped a fingernail to my wineglass and Pierre obliged. "Guy lived in town," I said. "So why was he staying at the hotel?"

"That's the funny thing. He often ate here, everyone does off-season. Willie's like a god in the chef-ing business. Knows twenty three ways to fix lobster."

And I vowed to try every single one of them. If I grew claws and got the urge to swim around in a tank in the supermarket, I'd have only myself to blame.

"But Guy never stayed here before," Pierre continued. "He took a room three weeks ago. Been coming and going ever since."

Interesting. "I heard he got fired from his job selling insurance, so he wasn't hustling to work. Where was he going?"

"No idea, but no place fancy. He wore the same clothes every day. Amy in housekeeping told me she noticed his suitcase was empty."

Pierre lifted the bottle but this time I declined. I needed to think, and I needed to be relatively clear headed to do so.

"Not now. Tuck the bottle away for me." Then I dropped the best exit line in movie history. "I'll be back."

I ended the day where I'd started it. Walking on the beach.

I played tag with the surf, squished into wet sand, and put my little gray cells to work. Antoinette Picasso sometimes played the diva, but the real me, Lynnette Cowler, came from hard-working prairie stock and never arrived on set unprepared. I studied those scripts end to end, scouring the clues, trying to guess the killer. I'd learned a thing or two about detecting along the way. If I thought of this puzzle as an episode I was about to shoot, perhaps I could figure out the mystery of Guy Hurt's death.

An aggressive wave chased me up the beach. I looked up to see Chief McGrumpypants glaring at me as if I was an escaped prisoner he'd just cornered. He was dressed in official mode this time, windbreaker and uniform pants that fit him like a glove. Cliché, I know. Sue me. I'm an actress, not a writer.

"Heard you've been asking a lot of questions in town, Mrs. Feathertop," he said when I caught up to him.

"See, Chief, now you're just being annoying."

His lips pulled back, flashing a fine set of pearlies. A smile. Maybe. "Care to tell me what you found out?"

What a faker. He already knew, but, hell, I'd play along. "Walk with me." He fell into step beside me. "I found out Guy was a son of a bitch bastard. No surprise. He had to be, for someone to want to kill him when he was already dead. Couple of angry ex-business partners hauling him into court. Several people he owed money to. A host of townsfolk who might've done him in. Including any number of women he loved and left. Am I even close?"

He grunted, which I took as a reluctant yes and I went on.

"He had a room at the hotel, though he was unemployed. He had a suitcase, but it was empty. He came and went at odd hours."

We'd come to a jetty. Well, what the locals called a jetty. I called it a tumble of barnacle-coated death rocks repeatedly slapped by frigid waves. Chief McBillygoat scrambled right on up there then shot me an *I dare you* look.

I hesitated. I could almost hear my calcium-deficient bones crack and the *ka-ching* of my orthopedics' cash register just looking at those slimy stones. But Antoinette Picasso never turned down a challenge, so I scrambled up after him. Okay, scrambled was a hopeful word. More like strained and grunted, feeling like the explorer George Mallory struggling up Everest, despairing of ever reaching the top. I declined the chief's outstretched hand. I wanted to do this...no, *had* to do it myself.

And then there I was, on the jetty.

Such a fine place to be, with a view of the water sparkling in the sun, boats bobbing at anchor, a sail on the horizon, and gulls cawing overhead. A breaking wave slapped the rocks and cold spray sprinkled my face. I breathed it in, feeling alive and invincible. And free.

The chief eyed me with an unsettling amount of admiration. Or maybe that was indigestion. Who could tell?

"Now it's your turn to share," I said, trying to catch my breath. "How'd Guy die?"

He swiped sea spray from his whiskered chin. "Why are you so curious?"

"Playing a detective for nearly fifteen years gets under your skin. You know I'm an actress, don't you? You must've checked me out. Eliminate the suspects, right? You probably also know my name's—"

"Mrs. Featherington." He tipped his head east, toward the end of the jetty. "We going on?"

The rocks got sparser there, slicker, and speckled with gull poop. A real challenge. I remembered that Mallory died on Everest. Better not push my luck.

"Not just yet," I said and we made our way back to the beach.

We fell into step again, as easy as if we'd been crunching along the sand together for twenty years.

"Come on, don't hold back, Chief," I said after a bit. "What killed Guy?"

"Heroin."

"He overdosed?" That was breaking news. "Why stab him? Throw him out the window?"

"No idea. The woman you saw might give us a clue. But I'm having trouble getting an ID on her."

"How about his hotel room? Did you find anything useful?"

"Hard to find anything. The place was tossed."

"But you found something." I could tell by his voice. All those years studying character quirks paid off.

"Things that make no sense. A couple of shriveled balloons and a, uh, nursing bra."

He looked adorably vexed, but for me, something clicked. "I might be able to make sense of it."

"You Mrs. Featherfern?"

"You're pushing it, Chief McSmartypants. Look, I think I know who the mystery woman is." At least, I hoped. "Meet me at the hotel bar in an hour if you want to find out. Now, I really must dash."

And then I did, because Antoinette Picasso not only knew how to make an exit, she also knew how to leave her audience wanting more.

———

Showered and changed for the second time today, I reapplied my makeup. Rays from the setting sun streaked through the lace curtain framing the window and glinted off the bathroom mirror. Something below the medicine cabinet caught my eye. Of course. Another tumbler clicked into place, like the combination on a safe.

I had the answer. Now I just needed to see the chief.

Pierre was all smiles when I got to the bar, but I told him to hold off on the wine. Didn't have to wait long for Chief McMuscles to scowl his way into the room. He wouldn't sit down, just stood there in a cloud of get-on-with-it gloom.

I realized I didn't know his name. Could've asked someone. It was probably listed on the town's website. But I kind of liked the mystery, as if he was a super-hot character on my show with eyes only for me, and not what he probably was, some old married guy with ten grandkids, a mortgage, and bunions. I did *not* want to know.

I asked Pierre to ask one of the waitresses I'd seen earlier to come over.

"Chief, meet Dolly Warren. Your mystery woman."

So much fun watching his startled gaze settle on her flat chest, not so much at the accusing look he turned on me. "You're wasting my time, Mrs. Featherthing."

Featherthing? Really? "I don't think so. This is the woman I saw going into Guy's room. That bra you found? It was stuffed. You stuffed it, didn't you, Dolly?"

She hung her head. "I-I did. I wanted Guy to like me. I liked him so bad, and I saw the girls he went with." She folded her arms across her non-existent bosom. "I just couldn't compete."

Chief McSofty went all fatherly, like he wanted to assure little buttercup she was beautiful as is, but I recognized a bad actor when I saw one.

"Cut the crap, Dolly. You and Guy were dealing drugs. Specifically, heroin. You were his mule. Picked up the drugs from a boat somewhere, filled a couple balloons with the heroin packets, and stuffed the balloons inside your bra. Then you came to the hotel. Brilliant mode of transport, and most likely no one would remember your face because their attention would be elsewhere. Especially men."

She looked stunned and impressed. Shouldn't be. When I put the pieces together, I realized the plot was almost identical to episode #11-15, *When the Cake Falls*. Proving, once and for all, there really are no new ideas.

"So, what happened?" I asked. "You two fell out?"

She nodded, somber. "The last shipment I brought, he told me we were done. He was taking off to Portland with Wendy. That son of a bitch used me. Told me he loved me, and if I did what he asked, we'd cash in big and go live somewhere warm. It was all a lie." Her dark eyes flashed. "I was *pissed*."

"Angry enough to kill him?" I asked.

"Didn't have to. Went to his room after my shift ended last night to have it out and found him sitting there. Dead."

The chief nodded. "Dealer got hooked on his own poison, and it took him out."

"Dolly, he was dead. Why'd you stab him?"

"I told you. I was pissed. I grabbed a knife off his room service tray and..." She grunted. One grunt was worth a thousand gruesome words. Fury, meet a woman scorned. "Then I left."

"Not before you searched for the drugs," I said. "You knew Guy transported the merchandise you brought to him in his suitcase, but didn't know where he hid it until he moved it. You tossed the room, looking for where he'd stashed the goods, but no luck."

Another grunt. Girl was a master communicator.

"Then you chucked him out the window," the chief said, wrapping it up.

She gawped. "Hell no. I work out, but I'm not that strong." She pulled her order pad from her apron pocket. "Can I go now? I got tables waiting."

I could practically see the steam coming out of the chief's ears. "No, you can't go now. I'm arresting you."

Minutes later, the dinner crowd watched as Officer Donnie perp-walked Dolly out of the dining room. Then they went back to their lobster primavera, and I thought about that bottle of Shiraz, but there was still one more loose end to tie up.

"Would you like to go upstairs?" Color the chief surprised at that one. "I mean to Guy's room. I think I know where he stashed his stash."

He agreed and steered me toward the elevator.

"Looks like Guy messed with the one doll he shouldn't have," he said while the car lumbered upward.

"Very clever, chief."

"Thank you, Mrs. Feathertree."

The bell dinged and the doors slid open. A moment later we stepped into Guy's room. I led the chief to the bathroom.

"Remember when men used razor blades? Back before stubble and scraggly beards became the fashion and men actually shaved?" He nodded and I had to admit, a little bit of whisker on that lantern jaw was kind of sexy. "Anyway, look inside. I think that's where the dope's hidden."

He pulled out a penlight. Prepared, I liked that in a man. He directed the light through a slit in the wall, under a helpful sign that read *Used Blades Here*. He gripped the mirror and wiggled the medicine chest, like testing a loose tooth, then eased the cabinet from the wall. There, amidst hundreds of discarded razor blades dating back to Prohibition, were dozens of small bags filled with drugs.

"Damn. My men missed it." He gazed at me. "But you found it."

That admiration-slash-indigestion look flashed across his face again. Now, Mrs. Featherpatch would have some sassy quip ready, music would swell, a-a-a-n-n-d *cut!* But me? I was a disaster without my writers. All I could do was stammer and blush. Like a giddy teenager.

"One thing you haven't solved, Mrs. Featherstairs. Who threw him out the window?"

"No clue." We headed for the door. "Grill Dolly some more. She's already up the river for drug dealing. She might confess to cut a deal—"

I broke off with a gasp and froze. The Norman Bates-clone busboy filled the doorway. Well, not quite *filled*. Not even remotely, he was so skinny. But the fact was, he blocked the way, with something gun-shaped jammed into his jacket pocket.

Pointed at me.

"Careful son. Think hard on what you're about to do," my companion warned.

"I know what I'm doing." Norman's voice squeaked with nerves, negating his entire argument. "You need to let Dolly go. She didn't mean to hurt anybody."

Oh, dear. "You're in love with her," I said, to which the chief rolled his eyes. "Did you, uh, help Mr. Hurt exit the building via the window?"

The guy's Adam's apple bounced like a bobber signaling a fish snagged on the line. "I did it to help

Dolly. I know she killed Guy, but I thought maybe the police would think he jumped. Me and Dolly, we go way back, but she keeps running off. I thought she might, you know, stay with me for good if I covered for her."

Poor kid. And nope, I wasn't going there with the parallels to my own life. Not anymore.

The busboy took a step. "Sorry, but if you don't let Dolly go, I'm gonna..."

Chief McHero tried to crowd me out of the way, but years of fight-training kicked in and I Jackie Chan-ed Mr. Bates into oblivion. The kid thudded to the hallway carpet before the chief could even put up his dukes.

He hustled over and took my arm. "Are you okay?"

"Yes." My head spun from my ninja adventures. "Uh, n-o-o-o."

He caught me before I could join Norman Bates on the carpet. I guess I wasn't all right. Goodness, who knew a tough old bird like me could faint? Before I knew it I was in a chair—hopefully not the one Guy expired in—with Chief McAttentive kneeling beside me, fanning my face.

"Toni, are you all right?"

"Yes. Pay no attention to my girlish vapors. Wait, did you call me Toni? So you do know who I am."

He puffed up. "I have a confession. I knew who you were the second I saw you. I'm a big fan of your show. Not the police work, it's all wrong. But I like the show. And you."

"Oh." I fluttered my eyelashes. "And is Mrs. Chief also a fan?"

"There is no Mrs. Chief. We split five years ago." He stood. "There's not even an auditioning to be Mrs. Chief at the moment. That role's yet to be cast." He held out his hand. "Come on, let's get you something to eat. You need to get your strength up if we're going to walk to the end of the jetty tomorrow. *If* you're ready to tackle it."

I grinned. Why, yes, maybe I was ready. I took his hand and let him help me up. We moved to the door. "Forgive me for asking an intimate question," I said as we stepped around the unconscious busboy. "But do you have a name?"

"It's Tom. Tom McManus."

More grinning. Tom and Toni. I liked the sound of that. "Tell me, Tom McManus, do you like lobster?"

"It's my favorite food."

"Chief, I think this is the beginning of a beautiful friendship."

MRS. FEATHERPATCH
& THE CASE OF
THE SKEWERED HAM

Mrs. Featherpatch is back and she's as sassy and snarky as ever. When the chief asks her to star in an amateur murder mystery production for charity, she doesn't expect to be upstaged by a real life murder.

"I DON'T KNOW HOW I ever let you talk me into this."

"You can't chicken out now," Tom said, steering his Jeep Patriot down one of Kindness, Maine's steeper hills, slick with snow and sleet. "You go in there, stab someone, and you're done."

He shot me a wicked grin that made my ancient heart go pitter-pat. Tom McManus, chief of police in this tiny seaside town, tall and buff and a teensy bit gruff, could talk me into anything.

Up to and including committing murder.

Well, not a real murder. He'd sweet-talked me into starring in a fundraiser for one of his aunt Honoria's many charities, a dinner theater murder mystery set in an English country manor, circa 1928. Me, Antoinette Picasso, longtime star of TV's *Mrs. Featherpatch Cooks Up a Murder*, winner of three Emmys, two Golden Globes, and one Golden Raspberry award, playing a murderer at a ham and bean supper, twenty bucks a plate.

During a snowstorm.

Oh, did I say snowstorm? I meant, a fricking nor'easter. In October.

It was for a good cause, I guessed, the town's historical museum. Don't get me wrong, I loved history, but if it wasn't for Chief McSexy's wicked smile, I'd be watching the storm ravage the Maine coast from the warmth and comfort of my hotel room. With him by my side.

"Tom, are you sure the show will even go on in this weather?"

He just smirked.

"The entire state of Maine seems to be snowed in," I warned.

He smirked again.

"We won't have an audience of more than three people," I insisted.

I got the third in the smirk trifecta as he turned into the parking lot. It was packed full of cars. I mean, bumper to bumper, practically stacked on top of one another.

Tom laughed, no doubt at my shocked expression. "We're Mainers, Toni, we don't let a little weather stop us."

"You know, there's a reason us flatlanders call you Maine-iacs."

"Not to our faces," he said. "Admit it Toni, you're coming to love Maine."

True. Since we'd met last spring, I'd practically lived here. I was even looking to buy a nice little summer place for when I wasn't working. Tom was a big part of that, but seriously, where else but Maine could a lobster addict like me spend her golden years? *If* I could make it through the winter.

Tom popped out of the Jeep and opened my door. We leaned into the wind-driven snow, sleet, and maybe even a little hail, and slip-slid up to the hulking old Grange building that had been converted into the Kindness Historical Museum.

Tom helped me up the steps, which had been salted and sanded but were still somewhat slippery. We entered a spacious hall with a high ceiling, wide floorboards, and pictures of the town's forefathers dotting wood paneled walls. The place smelled of ham roasting and beans baking. Rectangular tables ringed the room, jammed with people chatting, laughing, sipping red wine out of plastic cups and nibbling on cheese cubes speared onto toothpicks, as if the storm of the century wasn't raging outside.

Tom took my coat and hung it on a rack stuffed full of LL Bean's finest outerwear. His aunt Honoria, a spry elderly lady who could fit into my pocket, bustled up to us, twittering like a sparrow on speed. I put her age between seventy and a hundred, couldn't be sure and didn't want to ask. One never asks a lady her age if one wants to stay in good with the family.

"Oh, Toni, thank you so much for doing this," she bubbled. "When Tom told me you'd volunteered to be in our little show, I was beside myself with excitement."

I was drafted, but didn't argue the point. "This is quite a turnout, considering everyone needed dogsleds and snowshoes to get here," I said.

"They've all come to see you. I'd like to introduce you to everyone before the show, if that's okay. Oh, you're not hungry are you? We won't be serving for a few minutes, but the kitchen will make up a plate for the cast."

I held up my hand. "I'm good. I had a lobster roll before coming."

"Two lobster rolls, I believe," Chief McTattletale said.

I shushed him. Guilty as charged, but did the whole world need to know about my lobster addiction?

I gave Tom a push. "Why don't you go make trouble someplace else, while I meet and greet the fans. Honoria?"

She looped her arm through mine and led me around the room, stopping at each of the tables so I could chat, pose for selfies, and autograph programs, shopping lists and random slips of paper.

Some celebs—like my ex—would rather have their eyes poked out with a stick than get up close and personal with the general public. I was not one of them. Happy fans meant good ratings, good ratings meant a renewal and a renewal meant job security for me, an actress who had the gall to be over sixty in a profession where woman weren't encouraged to age beyond thirty.

Besides, all the *ooh-ing* and *ahh-ing* fed my voracious ego.

As I schmoozed, I looked around for my castmates. They were easy to spot, as they were already in costume, dressed up like they were at a 1920s *Downton Abbey* dinner party.

The man playing the vicar, a youngish guy with a beard and a brushy mustache, hunched over a table, shoveling in a plate of beans. The butler, an Abraham Lincoln clone minus the beard, lurked near the fireplace. He shot a death stare at a handsome piece of man meat in a dress suit and hair so shiny I could see my reflection in it. Mr. Handsome stood with two women in flapper get-ups, both blondes. The younger sported a fringed dress that barely covered her unmentionables, the older wore a headband with a feather.

The trio weren't very friendly. In fact, they were arguing. I listened in. Partly because I was nosy, but mostly because, as an actress, I sought to improve my craft by studying character and conflict. And there was a *lot* of conflict oozing out of that threesome.

"You *promised* me you'd leave her and run off with me," Younger Flapper whined.

"You promised *me* you wouldn't bounce any more bimbos between the sheets," Older Flapper cried.

Mr. Handsome laughed a monumentally nasty laugh. "I promise I'm gonna dump you both if you don't shut up."

Honoria sailed up and tugged me away before I could hear the exciting conclusion.

"Let's go elsewhere before that creep sees me," she said.

"Who? Mr. Handsome? What's your beef with him?"

She steered me toward the tables on the other side of the hall. "His name's Joey Brown. Cheats on his wife, cheats on his mistress, cheats his clients. And he's the world's pushiest real estate agent. He's been trying to get me to sell my land for two years. I've told him to leave me alone a hundred times but the obnoxious little shit doesn't take no for an answer."

Why were the ones who were good-looking on the outside so rotten on the inside? I glanced at

Chief McHunky, being fussed over and fed root beer barrels and other Depression-era candies by Honoria's elderly friends.

Except him. Tom was practically perfect inside, outside, and upside down.

I continued on, flitting from table to table. I signed and selfied and chatted until my temples throbbed and my cheeks ached from smiling. After what seemed like a decade, Honoria finally took pity on me and whisked me away to an alcove at the back of the room near the kitchen, where my castmates had assembled.

"Everyone, this is Antoinette Picasso," she said, breathless and impressed, as if announcing I'd walked on the moon. Which I'd done when I guest starred in SyFy channel's *Zombie Moonwalkers II*, but that was beside the point. "Toni, this is the show's director, Kevin Steel." She nodded to the Abe Lincoln clone. "And these are the rest of the Kindness Players. They volunteered to help out today too, like you."

Yeah, volunteered. If thirty-plus years of TV, film and stage work had taught me anything, it was how to read people, and the last thing this crew wanted to do was to be here. Especially that obnoxious little shit of a realtor and his flapper adversaries. They shot stinging glances at each other that brought new meaning to the phrase, *if looks could kill.*

Oblivious, Honoria ran through a quick introduction of each cast member. In addition to directing, Kevin had cast himself as the butler. Sally Seaforth, the young blonde flapper, was the ingenue, with Doug Dingle as the vicar. He was chowing down on more beans. I hoped they wouldn't kick in before the final curtain. We were in awfully tight quarters and I had a sensitive nose. Sally's *eau-de-cheap* perfume was already making me sniffle.

Next came Priscilla Plum, the forty-something blonde flapper, playing the dowager.

"I wanted to get cast in your role," she said, pouting at me.

And I wanted to sail into my golden years as a size two, but, as the Rolling Stones said, you can't always get what you want.

Honoria wrapped up the introductions with, "Last, and certainly least, Priscilla's husband, Joey Brown." She imbued the guy's name with maximum loathing.

I shook hands all around, even pouty Priscilla.

"Well, I've got to see to the dinner prep, so I'll leave you to it," Honoria said. "Break a leg, dearie." She hiked up to her tiptoes and gave me a peck on the cheek that made a jaded old cynic like me melt. Then she skedaddled.

"Honoria, wait," Joey called after her. "I wanna talk to you."

"Drop dead," she lobbed at him as she disappeared into the kitchen.

"Joey, can you keep your business affairs to yourself? My players need to concentrate," Kevin said with a considerable amount of acid. Or maybe that was bile. I could never keep those straight.

"Won't be *your* players for much longer, if I have my way," Joey said with an evil grin worthy of Simon Legree.

Kevin froze him with a glare and I added his name to the obnoxious little shit realtor's enemies list.

We did a short, extremely tense run-through of lines and blocking as the high school kids drafted into service delivered plates heaping with ham and beans to the audience.

Honoria had sent me the script, so I knew my lines, and everyone else's too. Kevin had written the play, creatively titled, *Murder at the Manor*. Basically an Agatha Christie rip-off. The bad parts Agatha had tossed into the circular file long before her work saw an editor. It was so terrible I expected the audience to flee the room and hurl themselves into a snowdrift to escape the second act. If the hammy performances didn't kill them during the first.

Run-through complete, Kevin tossed me my costume, a knee length sequined dress that had apparently been marinating in mothballs for a year. I navigated through the phalanx of teens clogging the steamy kitchen to the restroom to change. I nearly collided with Sally on her way out. She'd been crying.

I quickly donned my costume and headed back to the kitchen. I stopped short when I heard, "I could kill you for this." That was definitely the guy playing the vicar, Doug Dingle. He had a voice like a foghorn. Especially raised in anger like that.

I peeped around the corner and saw him near the ice machine, another plate of beans in his hands. Goodness, I did *not* want to be around when that gas giant went supernova. But I *did* want to be around for this explosion.

"That house you sold my mother?" Doug said. "The stairs *collapsed*. She'd only been there a week. She broke her back."

"Listen, Doug. These things happen, it's the price of home ownership." Joey's voice was as smarmy and oily as my agent's when he tried to convince me guesting on *Naked & Afraid* was a great career move.

"You *knew* it was a dump," Doug snarled. "*You* talked her into it when you knew the place was falling apart. She broke her back, man! You gotta make it right."

Joey laughed. "Not gonna happen. *Caveat emptor*, as they say. Buyer beware." He stiffened and sliced a glance at me. "Did you get all that

Mrs. Featherpatch, or do you want me to raise my voice?"

Goodness, he really was a little shit. I stepped into the kitchen, smoothing my dress. "No, I can hear you just fine, unfortunately."

Kevin stood at a mirror over a small sink in a corner, dragging a comb through his wavy hair. "Put your argument on hold, fellas," he said, turning to the bickering boys. "Put everything on hold. We've got a show to put on, and that's the only thing that matters."

Spoken like a true trouper. Or an anxious director who didn't want his actors to ruin his masterpiece of a play with their quarreling. Doug and Joey grumbled their way out of the kitchen, sniping at each other the whole time. Kevin gestured for me to go first, then followed me from the room.

Back in the main hall, the cast assembled on our makeshift stage, the open area in the center of the room, and we took our marks. The crowd buzzed with excitement. Honoria waved to me from her table, the seats filled with the cast of

The Golden Girls, plus Tom, looking outsized and uncomfortable in that sea of gray hair and pastels.

The teen volunteers drew the drapes across the windows. The house lights went out, the spotlight flared on. Jazz-age music from a boom box set the scene, wild applause greeted my first line, and the story of Lord and Lady Crumblebumble's ill-fated weekend party began.

Creaky dialogue and even creakier exposition laid out each character's conflicts and motivations with the subtlety of an elephant stomping into a tea party. The acting was overwrought, except Sally, who was pretty decent. Clearly Joey had ingested an entire hog before donning his tuxedo—he was the biggest ham who ever trod the boards.

Next to me, of course. I threw myself into the role of Lady Crumblebumble so hard it was a wonder I didn't hurt myself. I never got to play the killer, and I emoted the part with theatrical relish.

The end of the first act neared. The moment came when the spotlight would turn off then back on, and I'd be found standing over my husband's body, who'd been skewered by a knife to the heart.

The knife was really just a toy that Joey, playing the murdered Lord Crumblebumble, would squeeze in his armpit, but it'd do. Not like we were working with a Hollywood scale mega-millions budget.

Various threats to kill Lord Crumblebumble were delivered, the music faded out, thunderstorm sound effects piped up—couldn't have a cliché manor house murder without a cliché storm—and the spotlight winked out. Our ingenue Sally screamed, on cue. She'd scream again in roughly twenty seconds and the light would pop back on.

I had to hurry. I heard Joey crashing about as he got into place on the bar table where I'd find him spread-eagled and dead. I waded through the dark toward the sound. I brushed against someone, probably an audience member racing to the can, but I didn't let it disrupt my focus. Just ahead, Joey gasped and sighed, his death gurgle the most convincing acting he'd done the whole show.

I found the table. Quite painfully. I bashed against it, lost my balance, and fell, flailing in the darkness. Sally screamed again. The spotlight popped on. And there I was, belly-flopped on top of that obnoxious little shit of a realtor.

I blinked at the knife inches from my nose. It wasn't a toy. It wasn't in Joey's armpit. And Joey wasn't acting. He sprawled on the table, his tuxedo jacket open, blood sopping his snowy white shirt, his eyes lifeless and staring—and a carving knife sticking out of his chest.

I gasped. Joey Brown was dead.

———

Tom found a chair as far away from the body as possible and pushed me into it. He shoved the glass of water Honoria had given him into my hand.

"Sit, stay," he said as if my name was Fido, then he strode back to Joey's corpse. He stalked around the body like a lion on the hunt. He yanked his phone out of the back pocket of his jeans and dialed his detectives or the state police, or whomever the state of Maine required be brought in to investigate a murder.

I drank my water, agreeing with the *sit* part of Tom's command. I was too shaken up to stand. Numb, a little fainty, even. I mean, Mrs. Featherpatch found a body nearly every episode. Last count, she and her sensible shoes had stumbled over five hundred corpses, murdered in nearly as many ways. But me? Except for the occasional wake, I generally steered clear of the dearly departed.

"How are you feeling?" Honoria asked, gently squeezing my shoulder.

I drank the last of my water. "Better, thanks."

She wrung her hands. "Who do you think did such a thing?"

Ah. That was the question. I scanned the room. The once buoyant audience now sat subdued at their tables. The wait staff clustered near the fireplace. The Kindness Players gathered in the alcove. Everyone seemed to be in shock, but one of them was faking it. One of them was a killer. A real cold customer. Daring too, to stab a man with a hundred people in the room. What if the spotlight had come back on a few seconds early?

"I don't know, Honoria, but from what I saw and heard today..." I looked toward the alcove again.

"There were quite a few people who didn't like the man."

"What happened? Do you want to talk about it?"

Not really. I'd already told Tom and I knew I'd have to go over it again for the investigators. But I guessed I should get my story straight, so I ran over my role in the gruesome affair in as much detail as I could remember. I left out the part about Joey's death gurgle. I would be hearing that in my sleep from now on. And when I was awake.

"I hurried to hit my mark in the darkness, heard Joey crash onto the table, then brushed against someone before... Well, you know the rest."

"That person you bumped into has *got* to be the killer. Could you tell if it was a man or a woman?"

I rubbed my throbbing temples. "I don't know. It happened fast, and I was focused on getting to Joey—" Something popped in the back of my brain. Not an aneurysm, thankfully, but a memory. I stiffened. "Honoria, I think I know who the killer is." I bounced out of my chair. "I have to talk to Tom."

I hustled across the room and she followed.

"Yeah, see you in fifteen minutes," Tom said, ending the call and shoving his phone into his pocket. He directed a scowl at me. "Thought I told you to sit." He shifted that glare to Honoria. "And I told *you* to keep an eye on her."

I waved off his concern. "Do you always have to play Chief McBossypants?"

He grit his teeth in a give-me-strength way. Tom wasn't fond of my teasing nicknames, so of course I lobbed them at him every chance I got.

"Listen, I wouldn't be sticking my nose in if it wasn't important," I insisted. "I think I can help you solve the case."

That earned me an eye roll. "This is real life, not your TV show."

"Now, now. All these years playing Mrs. Featherpatch, I learned a thing or two about detective work. For instance, the knife, the murder weapon, it came from—"

"The kitchen," he finished. "I already checked. There's a carving knife missing." One side of his mouth quirked, practically a smile from Chief

McGrumpy. "Seems I know a thing or two about detective work too, Mrs. Featheringshire."

My turn to grit my teeth. I despised his teasing nicknames for me only a little less than he did mine. "Do you want to hear what I have to say or not?"

He shrugged, but I knew he was interested.

"I remembered something about the person I brushed against in the dark. A detail that can help pinpoint the killer."

Tom shifted into cop mode. "What? You know who it is?"

"Not exactly. But if I can talk to my castmates for a few minutes, I'll know for sure."

He brought out his scowl again. "You mean question the suspects, point fingers, tease out motivations, in other words, go full-on Mrs. Featherpatch."

"Why not? Who knows, you might have a confession before your investigators get here." I offered my most enticing smile. "Sound like a plan?"

"Sounds like a bad plan, but who am I, a highly trained officer of the law, to argue?"

He was goading me, but this wasn't the time or place for that. Later, when we were alone, he could goad me to his heart's content.

I turned to Honoria. "You want to come with?"

"Absolutely!"

"One question," Tom said. "What exactly are you going to ask that'll get a confession out a killer?"

"Oh, the questions won't matter. That's just a distraction." I took his arm and steered him across the room. "I'm going to find the killer by sniffing them."

———

I draped one of my TV character's comfortable cardigans over my shoulders—metaphorically, of course—and entered the alcove as Delphinia Featherpatch.

"Gather round, people," I said in her clipped, efficient way. I even clapped my hands.

The Kindness Players did as ordered, forming a circle around me. Sally dried her teary eyes with a paper towel. Kevin eyed me, rubbing his hands together. A dry-eyed Priscilla chewed on her pinky nail. And Doug shuffled over, eating a cookie.

"I have a few questions," I said, pacing around the circle. "Questions about Joey. Each of you here had a beef against him, each of you here had a reason to want him dead."

I stopped in front of Doug Dingle. His vicar's costume was stained with ham grease and bits of bean speckled his beard and mustache. "Including you. You had a hell of a fight with Joey in the kitchen, near the knives. I believe you threatened to kill him. Can you tell us what the argument was about?"

As he sputtered through an explanation about the collapsing stairs and his sainted mother's grievous injury, I got as up close and personal as I dared with a guy who'd eaten his weight in beans today.

Doug ended his tale of woe with the most clichéd line in all of detective fiction, "I didn't kill him, I swear."

I believed him. He passed the smell test. Failed the test, actually. I was looking for a particular smell, a scent I'd picked up on the person I'd brushed against in the dark. Joey's killer. And it wasn't Doug.

"What about you, Honoria? Joey had been harassing you. You went into the kitchen before the show. You had access to the knife." I gave her a sniff. Her scent was all old lady, lilac sachet and peppermint candies. "Where were you when the lights went out?"

Tom straightened. "Hold on, Toni."

"Hush, Tommy, it's a fair question," Honoria said. "Don't think it hadn't crossed my mind, dearie. Joey was a pesky fella, *always* bugging me to sell my property when I don't want to sell. Made me mad enough to spit nails. But I have eight acres on the oceanfront, and a dozen other realtors banging on my door too. I haven't murdered them, and I didn't murder Joey. I plead not guilty. At least, not guilty of *this* crime."

Tom did a double take and so did I.

"And for the record," she gushed. "I'm *delighted* you think I could be a murderer."

I let that hang, then swung on Sally. "What about you?" She twitched in alarm, making the fringe on her dress swish. "You were furious with Joey." I turned to Priscilla. "You too. I saw you both arguing with him earlier. What about?"

They exchanged glances, silent a second, then both volcanoes erupted.

"He told me he was going to leave her—" Sally jabbed a finger at Priscilla. "He was gonna run away with me and she was pissed. That's why she killed him."

"I did not. Joey told me he was going to dump you and come back to me. You killed him."

Neither one of them killed him. I had to abandon Sally's airspace because her perfume nearly knocked me over. I would've noticed if Joey's murderer had been drenched in that stink. And one sniff of Priscilla's whiskey breath let her off the hook too.

That left only one suspect.

"Kevin," I said, drawing out his name to several syllables.

"Chief McManus," he squeaked, shooting Tom a beseeching look. "Why are you letting her do this?"

Tom leaned against the wall and crossed his arms. "Because it makes you nervous." He nodded to me. "Please continue, Mrs. Featherlily."

I grinned. Oh how I loved this man.

I cleared my throat and started again. "Kevin, you and Joey had a tense moment earlier, something about the Kindness Players not belonging to you anymore if he had his way. What did that mean?"

Kevin gulped. "Nothing. It was a joke."

"It wasn't a joke," Doug said, munching on his cookie. "Joey was threatening to fire Kevin from the theater. Joey's on the board, uh, *was* on the board. He said Kevin was doing a lousy job as director."

"That's not true," Kevin blurted.

"Face it, Kev, you're no Spielberg," Priscilla said.

Sally nodded in furious agreement. "Ticket sales have been *way* down this season."

Honoria weighed in. "The board only made you director because you're Muriel's nephew and she's richer than Midas. You remember Muriel, Tom, she backed her car into the Cumberland Farms and you had to take her license away."

Tom grunted. He watched the action, all dour and scowly, but I suspected he was enjoying himself.

"You're all insane," Kevin cried. "That's not a reason to kill a man— Mrs. Featherpatch, what *are* you doing?"

Sniffing him of course. And getting my answer.

"Here's an interesting fact about me you don't know." I straightened Kevin's coat lapels and stepped back. "A long time ago I smoked. Forget drugs or infidelity, Hollywood's biggest scandal is there's so many smokers in the land of twelve-hours-a-day workouts and trendy juice cleanses. I quit when I got pregnant with my first child. Well, tried to quit. Nicotine is potent and addictive. Took me a full year to be free of demon tobacco."

Tom's eyes practically rolled out of his head and into the parking lot at that. *Get to the point*, he mouthed.

I did have a point, and it was a doozy. "Anyway, I kicked the habit, but to this day, twenty-five years later, just one sniff of that tobacco smell can ignite a craving so fierce my mouth waters. And *that's* what

I smelled when the lights were out. When I bumped into Joey's killer." I looked the murderer right in the eye. "When I bumped into you, Kevin."

I fell silent. Tom didn't say a word. Kevin's castmates glared at him with accusing eyes. Honoria pressed her palm to her mouth.

"All right, I killed him," Kevin said, his voice loud in the silence. "He was always lording it over me. In school, *he* was the quarterback. I was the water boy. He went to Bowdoin College. I ended up at Bates. *Bates!* He was a rich realtor, I'm a bank teller. And believe me, he didn't hesitate to rub it in." He glared at each of us in turn. "Then I got named theater director. For once in my life, I was better than him. I was on top. I was the director. He was just an actor. He was gonna take that away from me. I had to stop him. You see that, don't you?"

"Not really," Tom said, securing Kevin's hands behind his back with a zip tie he pulled from his pocket.

I followed the chief and his perp to the door, where Tom shoved Kevin into a chair to wait for the police to arrive. Sirens wailed from outside. They were close.

Tom turned to me. "You done good, Toni. And Kevin sure found out the hard way that smoking is bad for him."

"Never mind that, what's the deal with the zip ties in your pocket? Do you carry an emergency supply?"

"Have to, with you around. Bodies seem to drop at your feet. I like to be prepared."

"Seriously, Tom, you think it could happen again?"

"Maybe." He kissed me. "Probably."

I slid my arm around his waist. "Well, Chief, if it does, Mrs. Featherpatch will be there, and together we'll solve the case."

ECHOES

Vermont

Next stop is the Green Mountain State for an eerie tale of guilt and regret, and what happens when the ghosts of a woman's past come back to haunt her.

"THERE!" EDIE GILL GRASPED her great-niece Alice's slender wrist. "Do you hear it?"

"What, Auntie? I don't hear any—"

"Shush. *That*. It's water. Splashing. Can't you hear it?"

Alice tilted her head, appeared to be listening intently for a moment then focused her skeptical brown eyes back on Edie.

"Don't look at me like that, Alice," Edie snapped. "I may be ninety-five, but I'm not senile, and I'm not losing my mind. I hear splashing and what's more..."

She faltered, suddenly unsure. If she told Alice about the plaintive voice calling out to her, then her niece *would* think she'd lost touch with reality. A doddering and demented old lady who should be locked away in an old people's prison. And Edie would be damned before she ever agreed to go to one of those places.

"Now, Auntie, you know how the plumbing is in this old house. Maybe the toilet upstairs is running again. I'll go check."

Edie watched Alice hurry from the parlor with a sinking heart. Her great-niece was humoring her.

Alice didn't hear anything. But Edie did. Every day and each night for two weeks now.

Alice's spiked heels ticked across the wide floorboards as she headed toward the stairs. The splashing sound faded, but Edie thought she caught a dim echo of a girl's voice. Myrtle's voice. Her terrified cry for help Edie had tucked away in her memory over eighty years ago. She shivered. Could it be her imagination—or a guilty conscience?

Alice suddenly loomed by her side. Edie jumped and clapped a hand to her breast.

"I didn't mean to sneak up on you," Alice said. "I don't know what you've been hearing, Auntie, but I couldn't find any water running. Not even a drip." She peered at Edie with a troubled expression. "Are you sure you're all right? I don't like you living here in this cluttered old cave by yourself, in the middle of nowhere, with all this land around you and no neighbors for a good stretch. It's...creepy."

"We've been through this before, Alice. I will *not* move into assisted living. I'm doing fine on my own."

Better than fine. Edie was still able to go for a long walk every day. Oh, she couldn't explore her full twenty acres like she used to, but with the aid of a walking stick she'd whittled from a fallen birch branch, she could cover a lot of ground. She could still drive, even, and went twice a week to the senior drop-in center at the Brooksville church to play bingo and Parcheesi. Her hearing was still sharp, and so was her mind. Sharp as a tack, Dr. Vance said.

Until the last two weeks. Until Myrtle had come back to haunt her. Now Edie felt far from sharp, more like confused and unsteady. Like a helpless old lady.

Alice gazed around the dim parlor, lit by threads of sunlight that slipped around the edges of the drawn shades. She looked back at Edie and frowned. "My boyfriend Colton and me are thinking about buying a duplex in Middlebury, if we can scrape up a down payment. You could sell this place and come live with us."

Edie shook her head. "You're so good to offer, my dear, and don't think I'm not grateful for all you've done, but I couldn't. This has been my home since I was born, this is where I intend to stay until the end." And no ghost from the past was going to drive her out, no matter how much Myrtle tried. "Then this place and everything in it goes to you."

Alice brushed that off with a wave. "You know the most important thing to me right now is *you*. I'm worried about *you*."

"And I told you not to fuss," Edie said, growing weary and irritated. "I'm fine on my own."

"Okay. Whatever." Alice heaved a sigh. "I'm going to go pick up your groceries and when I come back I'll fix you dinner. How about pork chops?"

"That sounds nice, if you can get them on sale." Edie retrieved her old patent leather pocketbook from the table near the door. "Here, let me give you the money."

The putter of Alice's rattletrap Buick rolling down the long drive faded. Edie slipped off her loafers, put on her quilted slippers, and settled into the grooves worn into the seat of her old vinyl recliner. It was April, but chilly as usual in Vermont, and since she always kept the heat turned down to save on the bills, Edie huddled under three knitted Afghan blankets.

She reached for the TV remote on the table beside her chair. *Splash. Splash.* She froze. A muted, far away sound. *Splash. Splash.* She sat up straight, as if that would aid her hearing. The splashing turned to a deafening, desperate thrashing in an instant. Prickles of fear rose on the nape of Edie's neck.

"Edie, help me." Myrtle's voice. Terrified, echoing eerily. "Help *m-e-e-e.*" The cry cut off with a cough and a gurgle as if Myrtle choked on a mouthful of water.

Edie threw off the blankets and stood. "Go away, Myrtle. You're not real. Stop pestering me."

The watery flailing intensified and so did Edie's fear. She peered around the parlor, listening closely to the splashing and to the echoing cries. Where was it coming from? She inched toward the wall between the parlor and the kitchen and gingerly touched the lilac print wallpaper she'd helped Mother and Father put up nearly seventy years ago. None of the seams had matched back then and now the wallpaper was peeling and faded.

"Edie, why didn't you help me?" Myrtle wailed.

Trembling, Edie followed the voice. She slid her palm along the wall until she reached the oval mirror with the chipped gilt frame. Did the splashing seem louder here? She looked into the mirror, wary, fearing she'd see Myrtle's heart-shaped face framed by long, dark hair staring back at her. But all she saw was herself, an old woman with trench-like wrinkles cut into her face. Reminders of every laugh, every tear, every fear, and every sorrow that had touched her ninety-five years.

No sorrow was heavier than what had happened to Myrtle Doyle. Edie had spoken of it only a few times in her long life, but not a day had passed when the memory didn't cut through her heart. The memory of that terrible moment on the Muddy Branch of the New Haven River.

It was August and as hot as blazes. Edie wanted to swim down at the river. Her mother had forbidden it. Everyone knew you could catch polio from swimming, Mother warned, but Edie didn't take heed. She'd always been headstrong and willful, doing what she liked. She talked her best friend

Myrtle into swimming too. The trick was to tempt her with the boys Edie knew would be fishing near the old covered bridge. Myrtle was fourteen and boy crazy, so getting her to come along had been as easy as pie.

They'd swum out fairly deep in the cool, murky water, splashing around, feeling risqué in their slinky, one-piece swimsuits like Betty Grable wore in the movies. Then, something happened. Myrtle got a cramp or caught her leg in the tangled reeds just below the surface. She went under. She came back up, choking, struggling to tread water. She thrust out her arm, her hand grasping.

"Help me, Edie," she cried. "Help!"

But Edie hadn't helped. She panicked and swam away. The boys fishing nearby heard Myrtle's cries and dove in, cutting through the river with frantic strokes. Myrtle's strength waned and she sank like a stone. The boys reached her too late.

"Why did you leave me?" Myrtle's voice echoed accusingly in the parlor.

That question had dogged Edie her whole life. She'd almost convinced herself she'd abandoned

Myrtle to go for help, but deep down she knew...
She was afraid. Afraid she'd get in trouble for
swimming when she wasn't supposed to. Afraid that
Myrtle would drag her under. Afraid they'd both
drown.

"You should have helped me, Edie."

She narrowed her eyes. Myrtle's voice and the
splashing were louder here. It took some effort, but
Edie lifted the mirror from the wall and leaned it
carefully against the green vinyl hassock near her
chair. A dark oval stained the wallpaper, marking
the outline where the mirror had hung for easily
sixty years.

In the center of the oval, a shadow, an indistinct
outline, maybe a face. She gasped. Myrtle's face,
her expression contorted in terror, her eyes wide
and desperate. Edie placed her hand flat against
the fuzzy shape. It felt... Rough, almost three
dimensional. And wet.

"*Edie*," Myrtle shrieked.

Edie jerked away from the wall and screamed.
Terrified, she clapped her hands over her ears—and
fled the parlor as fast as her old legs could move.

Alice blew dust off the top of the antique terracotta lamp on the end table and turned the switch. A dim glow from a low-watt bulb lit the wall. Edie pointed and her niece squinted at the spot where the mirror had hung.

After a moment, Alice said, "I'm sorry, Aunt Edie, I don't see a face. Really, I don't. I think it's just water damage. Perhaps there was a leak and water pooled under the wallpaper. I bet it's that old toilet again. This is a stain, an optical illusion. Come to the kitchen, I'll make you some supper. And you can top it off with ice cream. I bought rum raisin, your favorite. You'll feel better."

Alice was right about one thing. Edie *did* feel better after eating. She kissed her niece good night, walked her to the door, secured the latch tightly, then curled up in her chair with her blankets and a big dish of rum raisin ice cream. She even found a rerun of *Murder She Wrote* to watch on TV.

With a full tummy, she saw things clearer now. Her imagination had been running on overtime.

Myrtle's death and the way Edie had abandoned her had stabbed at her every day. It was no wonder the guilt had finally caught up with her.

She polished off her ice cream, placed her dish on the table for Alice to clean up tomorrow, and settled back to watch the adventures of intrepid sleuth Jessica Fletcher. The sound from the TV washed over her and after a while, she dozed off.

Something icy and wet hit Edie's cheek and she snorted awake. The TV was off, the parlor dark and bone cold. Another frigid water droplet splashed onto her face. Groggy, she wiped her cheek with numb fingers and tried to focus her wavering vision. She stiffened in horror to see a shadowy figure standing over her. The apparition wore a one-piece bathing suit and water dripped from the long, bedraggled hair that hid its face.

"Myrtle?" Edie clutched her blankets and stared up at the undulating figure. "No. You're not here. You're not real."

"Why did you leave me?" Myrtle whimpered.

Edie caught the sound of someone flailing in water, muted, as if coming from a great distance.

She shuddered. Fear clutched her heart and terror filled her veins. This couldn't be. "I...I went for help—"

"You let me die."

"I was a coward," Edie whispered, reaching out. The movement made her head spin violently. "I'm sorry."

"Edie..." Myrtle drifted backward, wavering and shimmering, coming in and out of focus, her voice echoing. "You killed me, Edie..."

The TV popped on, the volume blasting. Edie cringed in her chair, hands over her ears, eyes screwed tightly shut.

"Coward. I'm a coward," she moaned over and over again, rocking back and forth as water splashed, the TV blared, and Myrtle's cries of despair rose and fell.

A long time later, someone grabbed Edie by the shoulders and shook hard.

"Leave me be, Myrtle."

"Auntie!"

Edie blinked rapidly and tried to focus on Alice, though her vision was still blurred and her head spun like an out of control merry-go-round.

"What's wrong, Auntie? You were tossing and turning like you were having a nightmare."

"A nightmare?" Had it all been a dream? It seemed so real. She touched her face—could that be river water on her cheek, or perspiration? She pushed the blankets off her lap and tilted her head. While Alice stared at her in alarm and more than a little fear, Edie listened, hoping to hear the sounds, but found only silence. No splashes, no cries for help.

Was she losing her mind?

"What are you doing here, Alice? It's not morning already?" She spoke more harshly than she intended.

"I realized I forgot my purse when I got to town," Alice said patiently. "I came back and found you in distress. Let me help you up to bed."

Alice reached out, but Edie slapped her hands away and rose from the chair on her own. It was a struggle, and she tripped over her blankets, but she managed to stay upright, though she still felt dizzy and disoriented. She tried to look for wet footprints or a puddle on the floor as her niece led her across the parlor, but her eyes refused to focus. Alice followed close behind as Edie slowly mounted the stairs, spooked by the creaks and groans that greeted each step.

A fine thing, when even familiar sounds gave her the jitters.

"Auntie, I'm taking you into Middlebury tomorrow to see Dr. Vance. And I don't want any argument." Alice helped Edie into her bed with the tarnished brass bedsteads. "You've been so jumpy lately. Perhaps he'll give you something to calm you down."

———

Dr. Vance examined Edie thoroughly but didn't tell her anything she didn't already know. She was in remarkable shape for a woman her age. He drew some blood, took her BP, checked her weight—up two pounds since her last visit—and at Alice's insistence, he checked her ears. Edie knew he'd find no medical reason for the eerie things she'd been hearing. And in the clear light of day, she refused to believe a ghost had been tormenting her.

It was guilt, pure and simple.

Guilt that had weighed heavily on her for eighty years. That terrible day Myrtle had died, Edie's life had also ended. She'd closed herself off from the rest of the world, locking herself away in her house, rarely leaving her property. Refusing to face the truth of what she'd done, refusing to move on, never letting anyone get close. Fearing if she did, she'd repeat the cowardly mistake she'd made with Myrtle and lose them too.

"Doctor, I'm worried about my aunt," Alice said, as if Edie wasn't in the room. "She seems so confused and fearful. She hasn't been sleeping well and now she's having nightmares."

"Stop fussing, Alice. It was one bad dream, that's all."

Alice sighed. "Is there anything you can do, Doctor?"

"I suppose I could prescribe sleeping pills to help you through a rough night." Dr. Vance gave Edie a reassuring smile, as if he was her father and not sixty years her junior. "But I'll tell you what I always tell you, Miss Gill, if you can knock off eating ice cream every day, you'll live another twenty years."

As she drove Edie home, Alice chattered about nothing. Edie didn't hear a word. She was lost in her tormented memories. When Alice's Buick bumped down the dirt lane and pulled up in front of the cottage, she expressed surprise that they'd arrived home so soon. Alice shot her such a concerned look, Edie decided to keep her confused thoughts to herself from now on.

"Are you sure you're gonna be okay?" Alice asked, helping her from the car.

"I'm fine," she snapped. "Now run along. You've given up enough of your time today. Your boss will be cross with you if you don't get back to work."

"Mr. Dowd can screw himself. *You're* what's important." Alice kissed her cheek, a quick peck, as affectionate as Edie would allow her to get. "I'll see you tonight."

The Buick tore back down the drive. Edie saw her niece light a cigarette before the car disappeared around the bend. Alice was a chain smoker but never lit up in Edie's presence. She was almost fifty and, though she'd had a string of boyfriends in and out of her life, Alice had never married or had a family. She'd put her life on hold to care for her. She took time away from her job at the bank, shopped for her, cooked dinner, and her crotchety old great-aunt repaid her by being waspish and mean.

Edie sighed. Just what she needed. More guilt.

She skipped her usual walk around her property. She was too tired. She went inside and made herself a tomato sandwich for lunch. Ignoring Dr. Vance's instructions, she dished up a generous two scoops of rum raisin ice cream for dessert. She settled in her chair and popped on the TV, eating her treat while watching a nature show on *Animal Planet*.

She dozed fitfully, waking after dusk to the sound of splashing. Myrtle moaned and called out, begging Edie to save her. Shadows danced across the parlor, making her head spin. Her old eyes wouldn't focus clearly and what's more, she found she couldn't move. It was as if she couldn't remember how to stand.

"Auntie, wake up."

"Myrtle?" Edie breathed, looking up at the figure bent over her.

"It's me." Alice's voice caught on a sob.

She tried to focus on her niece, but her head spun too much. "Alice. W-what time is it?"

"It's after six. I'm sorry I'm late but I had to work and make up the time for this morning, then I went to pick up your prescription." Alice's voice shook with emotion. "I heard you from the driveway. You were screaming for help."

"Oh." Had that been Edie screaming—or had it been Myrtle?

Alice shifted, looking nervous. "D-do you want some supper?"

Edie made a face. *Supper.* Her insides roiled. She couldn't eat a bite.

"How about some ice cream then? I'll go dish you some."

Alice turned toward the kitchen, but Edie grabbed her arm to stop her. She dug her fingernails into her skin.

"It's Myrtle. She's *here*. Don't you hear her?" Edie stiffened as Myrtle let out another wail.

Alice's expression tightened, turning fearful. "Auntie, you're scaring me. And you're hurting my arm."

"I'm sorry." Edie relaxed her grip and saw that her nails had left red half-moon indentations on Alice's wrist.

Alice made Edie a bowl of chicken soup. She wasn't hungry, but since Alice wouldn't leave her side until she'd devoured every drop, she scraped the bowl clean.

"Let's get you to bed," Alice said and helped her up the stairs, which was a good thing, since Edie's body sagged, bone tired and sapped of energy. Alice waited outside the bathroom while she washed up and slipped her dentures into the glass by the sink, and then her niece tucked her into bed.

"Here, take these." Alice held two sleeping pills in the palm of her hand.

"I don't need those. I don't like to take pills."

"Are we going to have another argument? Dr. Vance said they'll help you sleep."

Alice's voice went sharp, all patience gone, so Edie gave in. Honestly, she was too tired to put up a fight anyway. She swallowed the pills with a sip of water. Alice put the nearly full glass on the bedside table and Edie settled back against her pillow.

She listened to Alice's car rumble off—the girl needed a new muffler—then she closed her eyes to try to sleep. Her arms and legs grew limp. A warm, calm feeling seeped through her veins as the pills kicked in. Edie barely tensed when the splashing began. She let the sound cascade over her while she drowsed peacefully.

By the time Myrtle's ghost drifted through the door into the bedroom, Edie could barely keep her eyes open.

"Edie," Myrtle crooned. "Why did you let me die?"

Edie's head lolled and she struggled to form words. "S-sorry. Coward."

"You can make it right." Droplets of water dripped from her arm and splattered the floor as Myrtle pointed to the nightstand. "Take the rest of the pills, then come to me. I'll be waiting for you at the river."

Edie slowly turned her head to look at the pill bottle on the table beside her. It was nearly empty. She couldn't recall having taken so many.

"Don't be a coward anymore, Edie. It's the only way you can help me. The only way to save me."

"Yes...only way." Perhaps that was why Myrtle had come to her now. To tell her it was time for her to make amends. Edie tried to reach for the bottle, but she could barely lift her arm.

The floorboard creaked as Myrtle stepped forward. She snatched up the pills, shook two out of the container, and held them to Edie's lips. A shaft of moonlight spilled through a crack in the window shade and touched on Myrtle's wet face.

Not Myrtle. *Alice.*

The truth penetrated Edie's fuzzy mind. Frightened, and filled with disappointment, Edie tried to push her niece away, but she didn't have the strength. Alice shoved the pills into her mouth, pinched her nostrils, and yanked her head back. Edie pressed her lips together and tried to twist her head out of Alice's iron grip. Finally, the need to breathe forced Edie's mouth open. The pills sucked down her throat as she gasped for air.

Alice grabbed the water glass from the nightstand and dumped it into her mouth. Water splashed over Edie's face, into her nose and mouth. She gurgled and choked like a drowning woman.

Alice watched the EMTs roll her aunt's covered body out of the house on a stretcher, then she turned to the police officer.

"I came by to check on her as I do every morning. She was...she was gone." She glanced at the cop from under her lashes, hoping he'd buy her story. "I found the bottle of sleeping pills on her bed. She'd swallowed almost all of them."

The cop nodded as he scribbled her words onto his notepad.

"She was probably confused about how many pills she'd already taken," Alice said and dabbed her eyes with one of Aunt Edie's fancy lace handkerchiefs she'd kept tucked away in a drawer and never used. "I blame myself. She was so confused these days, seeing and hearing things. I knew it was dementia. I should've put her in a home long ago. But she was so independent, you know."

As soon as the police had gone, Alice opened the shades and curtains in the parlor. This house had been a cave far too long. She straightened the worn out sofa cushions, picked up the dingy blankets strewn across the floor and folded them, then she tidied the rest of the room.

The phone rang and Alice trotted into the kitchen to answer. She scowled at the black, rotary dial telephone hanging on the wall near the refrigerator, then picked up the heavy receiver.

It was Dr. Vance.

"I discovered one reason for your aunt's confusion," he said. "Her blood test showed the presence of psilocybin. Has your aunt been eating wild mushrooms?"

Alice smirked. "She hikes in the woods almost every day, and I've known her to eat wild berries, so maybe."

"Well, tell her to knock it off and she'll be fine. In fact, she could live for another twenty years."

Alice hung up. *She could live another twenty years*. She'd been hearing that since she was a kid. How could such a frail looking old biddy be so strong? How could she live so long? Alice had worried *she'd* be ninety-five before dear old Auntie finally kicked the bucket.

Before Alice could inherit everything.

She lit a cigarette and turned the heat up to eighty. She could do that now—this place was hers. Finally hers.

She went back into the parlor, to the image of a ghostly face she and her boyfriend Colton had burned into the wallpaper when Aunt Edie had been on one of her long walks. She peeled back the thin strip she'd secured over the hole Colton had cut into the wall. Good thing her aunt had been too rattled to think of doing that. If she had, she might've figured everything out.

Alice peered into the small opening. She could just glimpse the speaker in the darkness. Colton had hung it on one of the pipes. She reached in and pulled it out, thanking the techie geeks who'd invented wireless speakers and remote controls.

She and Colton had been able to turn on the splashing and moaning whenever they wanted. The hardest part had been pretending not to hear it. The sounds were pretty creepy.

No, the hardest part had been dressing up as poor, drowned Myrtle. She feared Aunt Edie would easily recognize her, so Alice had made sure to drug her by mixing mushrooms into her ice cream before she drifted into the parlor, dripping wet and her bedraggled hair in her face, moaning and wailing as Myrtle.

Alice thought she was done with the Myrtle act for good. But last night, though she'd dissolved several sleeping pills into her aunt's soup and her drinking water *and* made her take two more as she went to bed, Colton thought that wasn't enough to do the job. He'd insisted she dress up as the dead girl again, sneak into her aunt's bedroom, and force-feed her a few more pills, just to make sure.

Alice took a drag on her cigarette and blew out smoke in a long, satisfied exhale. The plan had worked—no more waiting for her crabby old aunt to die. Aunt Edie had rarely spoken about her friend who'd drowned and the guilt she felt, but she'd told Alice's mother long ago, who'd passed the story along to her. It was Colton's idea to use the sad memory against her.

The psilocybin in the ice cream had been Colton's idea, too. Alice couldn't even pronounce it. He knew all about that stuff, knew where to get all kinds of drugs. He'd said to slip Edie just a little, not enough for a full blown drug trip, but enough to guarantee confusion. And creepy nightmares.

Alice crushed out her cigarette in a crystal candy dish. As soon as she settled Auntie's estate, she'd have this old dump on the market. Not that anyone would want this ugly little house. They'd want the land. Twenty acres. Alice heard a cash register ding at the thought of the developers who'd be swarming this place.

She smoothed the wallpaper back over the hole and hung up the mirror. A sound startled her and she swung toward her aunt's battered old recliner. The dusty blankets were on the floor in a heap. Alice could swear she'd folded them.

Then... A gurgling sound, like someone choking on water, and the smell of rum raisin ice cream. A voice wafted through the room, wavering, echoing.

Accusing.

Alice shuddered. Aunt Edie's voice.

"Alice, why did you let me die?"

MURDER AT
<u>MIDNIGHT</u>

Connecticut

It's New Year's Eve 1942, and when the merrymaking turns to murder, plucky society reporter Sunny Harte puts on her crime beat hat to solve the case.

"Ten...nine...eight..."

The countdown to the new year had begun. The ladies and gents and various insurance men who'd gathered at Hartford, Connecticut's most exclusive country club shouted out the numbers in boisterous unison.

"Seven...six...five..."

Dressed in their finest glad rags, the crowd raised glasses spilling over with champagne that sparkled in the light from the ballroom's crystal chandelier, everyone eager to say farewell to 1942 and hello to '43.

Everyone except Millicent Rutledge.

Oblivious to the giddy celebration, Millicent burst from the crowd and did a spastic jitterbug across the room. She aimed toward the dessert table, where I stood trying to choose between an array of treats utterly devoid of strictly rationed sugar and eggs. She lurched closer, scattering dolled-up debutantes and men wearing starched shirts and smart tuxedos in her wake.

I gaped at her in shock and concern. Something was terribly amiss. Her moon-shaped face had gone as red as ripe cherries, her dark brown peepers bulged, and she clawed at her throat, gasping for breath like a guppy out of water.

"Four...three...two..."

I darted forward and reached to help her. Too late. Millicent toppled like a thick old elm tree and crashed onto the dessert table.

"...one. *Happy new year!*"

Party horns hooted and more champagne corks popped. The four-man brass combo in the corner launched into a swinging version of "Auld Lang Syne." People embraced, lovers kissed, and hopeful toasts were offered for peace in the coming year and an end to this dreadful world war.

And I stared in horror at poor Millicent Rutledge, sprawled across the table, face down in the punch bowl.

Dead.

———

Lieutenant Arthur Pell stared down at Millicent Rutledge as two sturdy men from the coroner's office pushed the stretcher carrying her sheet-covered body past him toward the exit.

"I should've known I'd find you in the middle of this."

The lieutenant wasn't speaking to the late Mrs. Rutledge. He directed that wry, slightly acid comment to me.

"What do you mean?" I asked, eyeing the lanky detective. His cheap blue suit and frayed trench coat were out of place in the country club's swanky digs.

"I mean, wherever there's a murder, I'm sure to find Sunny Harte."

He said my name with his usual smirk, garnished with a mocking chuckle. My name amused him and the rest of the policemen in his precinct to no end, but their ridicule didn't bother me. I'd heard every wisecrack in the book about Sunny Harte and had learned to live with the snickers.

"I hope you're not implying anything by that crack, lieutenant. You know my newspaper sent me to cover this shindig—" I stiffened. "Wait a doggone minute. Murder? Are you saying someone *killed* Mrs. Rutledge? It wasn't a heart attack?"

His smirk turned smug. "That's what I'm saying. Gotta wait for the coroner's report, but from my initial look-see, I think the old dame was poisoned."

I gasped. "Poisoned? How do you know that?"

He quirked an eyebrow so bushy a caterpillar would be forgiven for trying to cuddle up to it. "Give me some credit, Mrs. Harte. I've been on the job for twenty years." He touched a finger to the tip of his broad nose. "The nose knows, and this nose would know the smell of bad almonds anywhere. That could mean cyanide."

Cyanide? I watched the coroner's men ease the stretcher through the wide mahogany entrance doors and down the front steps. Icy winter air rushed in, muscling its way through the scents that hung over the room like a heavy cloud—perfume, champagne, and cigarette smoke. But *not* almonds. I hadn't caught so much as a whiff of almonds.

My mind whirled. Wealthy and often disagreeable, Millicent Rutledge was the type of rich relative to bump off quietly, smothered in her sleep by a greedy niece or nephew jumping the gun on their inheritance. Not poisoned. And not in such a public place.

Then again... After what I'd seen and heard tonight, it made sense. "Lieutenant, do you think one of the guests here is responsible?"

"I do. The right dose of cyanide is fast and fatal. If the dame croaked at the stroke of midnight, she must've been poisoned not long before. Everyone here is a suspect."

Pell cast a suspicious glance around the room. Soon after he arrived, he'd ordered everyone to stay put. Now, scores of party guests paced the dance floor under the glittering chandelier or sat at cocktail tables pushed up against the ballroom's gold paneled walls. The guests smoked, speculated, and spoke in low voices as they stared warily at the police officers who swarmed the room. Certainly not what the city's elite had expected when they'd coughed up the dough for the tickets to the country club's New Year's ball.

Not what I'd expected either. What had begun as an assignment to cover a fancy party doubling as a war bond drive, had now become a murder scene.

"Everyone's a suspect," Pell repeated. "And I've got to interview all of them." He gusted a put-upon sigh then looked at me. "Unless you can help me out. You were covering this affair. Did you notice anything unusual, anything out of the ordinary?"

"Besides Millicent Rutledge's swan dive into the punch bowl?"

His expression turned testy. "You're as funny as Fanny Brice. I meant *before* that. You must've seen something out of place. You're a reporter, aren't you?"

Nice of him to finally notice. I'd been straddling two beats at the *Daily Bulletin* since the war had started and a number of the newspaper's male reporters had joined up. I covered society news and the police beat, a challenging combination of fashion and fatalities.

The police—and particularly Lieutenant Pell—hadn't done much to make my job easy. Pell never returned my calls, and he greeted me at crime scenes with enough cold shoulders and chilly glares to give me frostbite. This was the first time he'd ever uttered the word reporter and my name in the same sentence. And the first time he'd ever asked for my help.

It felt good.

"I didn't see who poisoned Mrs. Rutledge, if that's what you mean. But... I did *hear* something unusual. Several unusual somethings, in fact."

He brightened. "Such as?"

I took a breath, about to push my luck. "Tell you what. I'll spill the beans on everything I know if *you* promise me an exclusive."

He looked at me like he'd rather promise me hard time on a chain gang, but he agreed. Resisting the temptation to crow in satisfaction, I fished a small notepad out of my beaded clutch purse. The lieutenant pounded his trench coat pockets until he found his own notebook and pencil then gazed at me in expectation.

"I was on alert for crimes of fashion tonight," I began. "But several things caught my police reporter's ear. They weren't the usual gripes about rationing and shortages, so I jotted them down. I heard Mrs. Rutledge quarrel with several people this evening. Now, talking to Millicent about the weather often turned into an argument. She was always spoiling for a fight. But these weren't her typical spats." I opened my notepad. "That's why I took notes. The disagreements seemed odd."

I flipped back a few pages and scanned the notes written in a hasty scrawl only I could decipher.

"The first potential suspect you should talk to is Bertha Gouch." I pointed discreetly to an elderly, frail-looking woman the exact size and proportions of a sparrow. She wore an old-fashioned floor-length Alice blue gown that made my outdated teal cocktail dress look positively chic. She'd swept up her long, steel grey hair into a turn-of-the-century Gibson Girl bouffant, a thick pile of hair that looked to outweigh Miss Gouch by twenty pounds.

"That sweet old lady?" Pell said. "She seems like she couldn't hurt a fly."

"If you'd heard what I heard, you might think differently. A couple of hours ago, Bertha stomped up to Millicent near the bar. She seemed agitated. That piqued my curiosity, so I stepped closer to the two women, and then I heard Bertha say..."

"I have a bone to pick with you, Millicent Rutledge."

"Good evening to you too, Bertha," Millicent said in a cool voice, her gaze sweeping the smaller woman head to toe. "My dear, you really should retire that gown. You've been wearing it since Roosevelt became president. And I am not referring to dear Franklin Delano, either."

Bertha's narrow, beaky face puckered. "Is it true what I hear? That you've put your name in for president of the Women's Club?"

"Absolutely true."

"But you know I've been president for thirty years. No one has ever run against me."

"But I'm not running," Millicent said. "You're going to resign, in favor of me."

Miss Gouch clapped a hand to her breast. "Resign? L-let you become president? Whatever do you mean?"

"I mean, the jig's up, old girl. I've always wondered why we pay such high dues to be members, yet the club's coffers are always empty." A satisfied cat smile spread across Millicent's puss. "I've discovered where the money's going. Into your grossly unfashionable purse."

Bertha blanched. "How d-dare you accuse me of—"

"I'm not accusing. I have proof." Millicent cackled in delight. "And isn't it interesting how your apricot jam always wins first prize at the club's annual fair?"

Bertha gulped. "Because my jam is the best jam in Hartford County."

"Your apricot jam could kill a goat with an ironclad stomach. You've been bribing the judges, using stolen dues money to secure the prize ribbon year after year. As I said, my dear, the jig is up. You've behaved like Hitler in a skirt long enough. It's time for a new dictator at the Women's Club."

"But Millicent," Bertha cried. "It's...the *club*. It's my whole life. It's *everything* to me."

"Not anymore." Mrs. Rutledge stepped closer, her height and size dwarfing the smaller woman. "You'll step down or I'll let the ladies of the club know your terrible secret. Won't they be surprised to find out that prim spinster Bertha Gouch is a common thief?"

Bertha trembled as if an earthquake shook the ground beneath her, but her voice didn't waver as she said, "I could kill you for this, Millicent. I really could."

"...I didn't hear her next words," I said, my gaze on Lieutenant Pell. "A fella who'd had one martini too many bumped into me, distracting me. But Miss Gouch seemed frosted for sure, maybe angry enough to poison Millicent."

"Apricot jam," Pell mused. "Cyanide can be extracted from fruit pits. You'd need a lot of pits, but, if she cans her own, then she's got access to the murder weapon."

He made as if to go nab the old gal, who twittered nervously near the bar, taking hearty swigs of champagne.

"Hold on a minute, Sam Spade." I tugged at his sleeve. "She's not the only one who might've wanted Millicent dead. There's Elmer Woodward."

"The grocery store tycoon?" Pell's attention focused on a man hovering at the door as if he'd like nothing more than to bolt. Shaped like a bowling pin, Woodward wore a crisp new tuxedo, the jacket open, and a gold watch chain stretched across his portly midsection.

"Seems Elmer Woodward is a traitor to his country," I said. Pell looked alarmed so I rushed to reassure him. "Not *that* kind of traitor. He's not a spy. He's a black marketeer. At least that's what Millicent called him." I flipped my notebook forward a few pages. "It started when Millicent snatched up a plate and cut into the buffet line between me and Mr. Woodward..."

"Good evening, Elmer," Millicent said. "Goodness, would you look at that lovely roast?"

She gestured toward the buffet and the succulent shank of beef carved by a burly man in a chef's hat. Mr. Woodward replied with a distracted grunt. He grabbed a slotted spoon and scooped up a generous helping of Victory-slaw, shredded cabbage and carrots soaked in vinegar.

"I'm surprised the country club could get such a portion of beef with rationing so strict," Millicent said. "They must've used their ration points for the entire year to secure that." A knowing smile stretched her red-painted lips. "Or perhaps they paid you a visit, Elmer?"

Woodward froze, eyeing Millicent warily. "What do you mean?"

She speared several slices of ham on her fork and dropped them onto her plate. Lowering her voice, she leaned closer to Elmer. I had to lean closer too, so as not to miss a word.

"I *know* you're active in the black market, selling rationed goods," she said in a hushed voice. "I *know* all about the deals you make to divert meat, sugar, canned fruit and all manner of rationed items to your friends. For a price."

"I have no idea what you're talking about." Woodward's voice remained calm, but he slapped the Victory-slaw onto his plate, clearly rattled.

"You know *exactly* what I'm talking about, Elmer. You've been selling the food supplies to the highest bidder, without a care for the rationing rules. When an honest citizen like me goes to one of your markets for meat and eggs, the shelves are bare. You've left us ordinary folks to starve."

The buffet line moved. His angry gaze raked over her as we all inched forward. "Lady, you don't look like you're in any danger of starving."

Millicent let out a harsh laugh. "I may be plump, but I'm not unpatriotic, nor a traitor to my country. I don't profit from this war. You've broken the law and I'm going to make sure you're exposed for it. There's a place for people like you, and it's called jail. I hope they put you away for a long, long time."

"Mrs. Rutledge..." Woodward spoke in a low, dangerous purr. "I advise you to keep your mouth shut or I'll shut it for you."

"...Millicent shook him off and toddled away with her dinner," I concluded. "She didn't take Woodward's threat seriously. Maybe she should have."

Lieutenant Pell's eyes narrowed as he gazed at Elmer near the door, practically digging a trench in the floor with his pacing. "If Mrs. Rutledge's accusation proves true, Woodward could face up to ten years in jail, a ten-thousand dollar fine, or both. That's a suitable motive for murder. But where would he get the poison? I like the old dame for the killer. Just got to figure out how she did it."

"There's one more suspect. Millicent has a daughter, Prudence." I nodded toward a curvy woman of about twenty-four with brunette hair styled in a mass of Shirley Temple curls. She sat near the far wall, eyes wide and vacant, seemingly in shock. "She's been walking out with the gentleman by her side, Marty Martin."

A wiry man roughly Prudence's age, Marty Martin wore a rumpled tuxedo, his tie askew and his thick brown hair in disarray. He stood next to the grieving young woman's chair, his hand resting on her shoulder.

"Mr. Martin met Prudence at her mother's company, Rutledge Exterminators. They both work in the sales department. Apparently, Mama found out about her daughter's office romance a week or so ago and she wasn't happy. I was returning from the powder room when I saw Mrs. Rutledge behind one of the potted palms. She was yelling at someone. I crept as close as I dared and spotted Marty Martin cringing in Millicent's shadow..."

"I know why you're wooing my daughter, Mr. Martin," Millicent said. "You're after my money. You know full well Prudence owns half of Rutledge Exterminators. You figure if you marry her, you can push me out and then you'll have it all."

"Did it ever occur to you that I might be in love with your daughter?" Marty said with admirable grit.

She sneered. "Ridiculous. Have you taken a good look at Prudence? She's not Greta Garbo. The girl makes Groucho Marx look attractive."

"That's cruel," Marty said in disbelief. "You're her mother, for Jiminy sake."

Millicent casually brushed lint from her shoulders. "And you are my employee. Not a very good one, I might add. Why couldn't you have gone off and joined the Army like every other man under forty?"

"I wanted to enlist. But I got flat feet. The Army, the Navy, all the services turned me down as 4-F."

Millicent snorted. "You may not be soldier material, but you've waged quite a battle to get my company through my daughter. That's over now and you've lost, young man. I'm ordering you to break it off with Prudence this instant. Return to the ballroom and tell her you're through or so help me, I'll destroy you. You'll regret ever coveting my business."

"I'm not after your business, or your money." He thrust a finger in Millicent's face. "Get that through your thick skull. I love Prudence and she loves me."

She slapped his hand away. "Love? Piffle! You're a liar, Mr. Martin, and I insist that you end this foolish scheme right now."

"No. I intend to be part of Prudence's life from now on. For the duration, as they say. I'm going to ask her to marry me. In fact, I'm going to ask her tonight."

Millicent huffed. "Over my dead body."

"What a swell idea," he spat, then stormed off.

"...That's it." I closed my notepad and stuffed it back into my purse. "Three arguments, three people with good reason to poison Millicent."

"A slick black marketeer, a dame with her fingers in the till, and a threatened lover," Pell said. "You know, you'd make a good spy, Sunny Harte." A hint of admiration cut through the usual smirk in his voice. "What about the husband? Where's Mr. Rutledge in all this?" He glanced around the ballroom. "I don't see any fella kicking up his heels at the old battleaxe's demise."

"That's because Phil Rutledge died a dozen years ago. He left his widow with a daughter, a mortgaged home, and a business deep in debt. Millicent turned it around. She was a smart cookie. Smart and ruthless. She built Rutledge Exterminators into a profitable company, with a chain of stores all over the state. She succeeded in a man's world. Probably why she was so eager to keep Marty away from her business."

"Exterminators keep all kinds of chemicals and pesticides on hand." Pell glanced toward the sad-looking lovers. "It would be an easy thing for Martin to pilfer some poison. But so could the daughter. She could've had her eye on the business too, and more than just half the profits.

She could've decided to give mom the bum's rush and hurry her inheritance along."

"Jeepers, I hadn't thought of that. All right, so now there are four suspects."

A long-legged redhead in a snug-fitting policewoman's uniform interrupted us, beaming with excitement. Peggy Callahan, the first woman to work on the detective bureau, the first policewoman on the entire city force, for that matter.

"Lieutenant, come see what I found," she said. "In a rubbish barrel, over at the bar."

———

Pell wrested a silk handkerchief from a bystander and used it to gingerly remove a small vial from a woven straw basket next to the bar. Holding the container to his nose, he jerked back.

"As I suspected. Almonds."

He thrust the vial in my face, and I caught the faint scent of almonds. I nodded at Pell, more than a little surprised. Was the gesture a sign he had finally accepted me? Or perhaps simply eager to show me that he'd been right all along?

"How'd this get in that bin?" Pell barked at the bartender, a slim, gray-haired man in a starched white jacket and bow tie who identified himself as Mack.

"Dunno." Mack shrugged. "It's been busy tonight. Anyone coulda tossed it in when I wasn't looking."

"I saw Millicent arguing with Miss Gouch near here earlier," I told Pell. "And Marty's been glued to that spot by the bar for ages. So has Prudence."

Pell nodded and asked the bartender to recall if any of our chief suspects had come by for a drink.

"Are you bats?" was Mack's reply. "It's a party. I seen everybody here tonight, 'specially that old lady with the bird's nest on her head. Never know it to look at her, but she's a real lush. Came up here five, six times at least."

"How about the dead woman?" I asked. "Did you make her a drink?"

Pell scowled, clearly annoyed I'd gotten to the question first, but Mack didn't miss a beat.

"Her I remember. The lady ordered three martinis and griped at me the whole time. Step on it, she says. Use Martini & Rossi vermouth instead of the bar brand, she says. Only one olive, she says..." He ticked off Millicent's demands on his fingers. "And get this, she spills one of the drinks, so I had to make another one. And after all that, she didn't leave a tip."

Pell's brow furrowed. "Three martinis? One for each of our suspects?"

"I don't think so." The puzzle began to take shape in my mind. "Mack, did Mrs. Rutledge carry the drinks herself?"

"No, some other dame helped."

"The boozing old lady?" Pell asked.

"Nah, a younger girl. Looked a lot like the dead dame."

"Prudence." The lieutenant got an *I've-got-you-now* gleam in his eyes. "She slipped her mother a fatal Mickey."

———

The lieutenant was ready to haul Prudence Rutledge out of her chair and off to the pokey as soon as he introduced himself, but I wasn't so sure she was the culprit.

"I'm sorry for your loss, Miss Rutledge," I said gently.

Prudence nodded solemnly, tears glimmering in her wide brown eyes, her expression strained with grief. If she were acting, as Lieutenant Pell seemed to think, her performance could rival Katharine Hepburn in any of her dramatic films.

"I'm confused," Prudence said. "Why are the police here? Why can't anyone leave?"

Pell peered at her keenly. "Because, Miss Rutledge, your mother was murdered."

Prudence gasped. "M-m-murdered?"

"I'm afraid so," I said. "Could you and Mr. Martin answer a few questions? The bartender says you helped your mother pick up some martinis. When was that?"

She tilted her head and frowned, apparently thinking hard, which made her look like a dyspeptic poodle.

"Just before midnight," she said slowly. "Marty had just asked me to marry him, and I accepted. He insisted we tell mother the happy news. When we did, she suggested we have a drink to toast our engagement."

Pell snorted. "You're lying. Your mother demanded Mr. Martin break off your romance. She threatened to ruin him if he refused. Why would she congratulate you on an engagement she didn't want?"

"Darling, is this true?" Prudence looked up at Marty, still standing next to her. He flushed guiltily.

"It doesn't matter, dumpling." Marty shot Pell a hard look. "Millicent's threats didn't bother me. I didn't care if she fired me. I could get another job *like that*." He snapped his fingers. "Every factory in the city's looking for help. Some are paying double or even triple what they did before the war. I didn't care what Millicent thought. I love Prudence and want to marry her no matter what."

Prudence's eyes brimmed with happy tears this time. "Oh, Marty."

"Did your mother ask for help with the drinks?" I prodded, getting back on track.

"No, but I saw that she'd spilled one and went to help her. Mother is... Mother *was* as clumsy as a toddler, you see. I knew she couldn't carry the glasses herself, so I rushed over to lend a hand."

"And you took the opportunity to pour a vial of cyanide into her glass," Pell said.

Prudence gazed up at him, blinking rapidly. "A vial of what?"

"You were angry because she wouldn't let you marry Mr. Martin. You poisoned her." Pell glared at Prudence's beau. "Or maybe you *both* conspired to kill her. With her dead, you'd have the business to yourselves. And all the dough that comes with it."

"That's absurd," Marty cried. "And absolutely untrue. Prudence wouldn't... I would never do anything like—"

"I believe you," I cut in. "Prudence, did you carry all three martinis from the bar?"

She nodded. "Yes. Mother gave them to me, said she'd catch up to me after she left the bartender a tip."

"Was there anything odd or unusual about the drinks?"

The gassy poodle look came over her face again as she considered my question. "Well, one drink had an olive. Mother was most particular Marty have that one. She was being thoughtful. I'm not partial to olives, but Marty adores them."

I doubted Millicent had ever done anything thoughtful in her life, no matter what her daughter might think.

I turned to the lieutenant. "Millicent Rutledge wasn't supposed to die. The poison was meant for Marty."

Pell stiffened. So did Prudence and her beau.

"The whole thing was Millicent's scheme. She deliberately spilled the drink. When the bartender turned his back to make another, she dumped the cyanide in the glass with the olive. She gave the martinis to Prudence then told her she was staying behind to leave a tip, which we know from the bartender isn't true. He said she didn't leave him a single dime. She really stayed behind to toss the empty vial into the barrel, getting rid of the evidence."

Prudence's Shirley Temple curls bounced as she vigorously shook her head. "Evidence? Poison? I don't understand."

"I'm sorry, Miss Rutledge. Your mother poisoned the drink herself. To kill Marty."

Pell scoffed. "But in a fit of remorse, the old dame decided to do herself in and swigged the drink down? That's a stretch."

"Not at all. Millicent came to me before she died, as if trying to tell me something. In her last coherent moment, she realized the drinks were somehow switched. That *she'd* drunk the one with the poison. The question is, was the switcheroo on purpose? Or an accident?"

I looked at Prudence, who'd suddenly gone as white as chalk, and knew the truth.

"Marty took a glass from me," she said haltingly. "But then I remembered what Mother said about giving him the olive. I'm... I'm afraid to say... Well, the olive was on a toothpick balanced on the rim of the glass. Instead of switching drinks, Marty simply plucked the toothpick off the other glass. When Mother joined us, *I* must've given her the one with the poison... Oh dear!"

She broke into heavy sobs. Marty bent down and hugged her.

"Oh dear is right," I said to Pell as we walked away from the tearful couple and crossed the room. "Millicent thought she could bully Marty into ending things with Prudence, but when he defied her by proposing instead, she saw no other solution but murder. Unfortunately, her scheme backfired with tragic results."

Pell frowned. "It can't be as simple as that. I still think the lovers had something to do with the dame's unhappy end."

"Look at them. Prudence is truly grief-stricken. Marty's more than shaken up. Realizing your future mother-in-law tried to kill you could do that. I bet when you test the fingerprints on that vial, you'll find only Millicent's. Don't forget, she had access to every chemical in her company and she probably knew exactly how to use them. I told you she was smart. Until fate and a couple of olives caught up to her."

Pell digested that a moment. "By gum, you figured it out, Sunny Harte."

No mocking when he said my name this time, and not a hint of a smirk. I beamed in delight.

"Look on the bright side, lieutenant. There's still two mysteries you'll get the chance to solve. Do a little digging. I'm sure you'll find enough evidence to arrest a shifty grocery store tycoon selling black market goods and an embezzling spinster." I touched his arm, stopping him before we reached the door. "And for your information, *I* plan to be there when you make both arrests."

He lifted one of those caterpillar eyebrows, a combination of dread and amusement.

I grinned. "I'm afraid you're stuck with me on the crime beat. For the duration."

THE HOT SEAT

Rhode Island

Let's wrap up our murderous mystery tour of New England with the shortest story, set in the region's smallest state. When a crooked antiques dealer tries to cheat a client, he soon finds himself in the hot seat.

FRANK FORD COULDN'T BELIEVE his luck.

When he arrived at the old lady's rundown Victorian mansion and began to pick through the lamps, knickknacks, and musty old books piled on bookshelves, Frank hoped he'd find something of value. That often happened when these older folks called his shop, *Frank's Finds & Antiques*, asking him to come look at their possessions. He found mostly junk, but sometimes he'd dig up an item worth a decent chunk of change, an antique teapot forgotten in a cabinet or a vintage copper saucepan doubling as a foot bath.

But he'd never in his wildest dreams imagined he'd find an original Howe Brothers chair stuck at the end of a hallway. Probably a hundred fifty years old, the chair was weighed down with a stack of old *Life* magazines piled on the seat. Except for some dust, the antique chair appeared to be in great shape.

And valuable. *Very* valuable. Frank knew that for a fact.

Celina Chouinard shuffled stiffly toward him.

"Did you find something of interest?" she asked. Ninety or maybe older, and with hair as white as the snow that fell outside, Celina's voice was thin and aged, mixed with excitement and skepticism. "Not the *Life* magazines. Do you honestly think anyone would pay money for those ancient things? There's nothing older than yesterday's news, you know."

"What?" He'd been so focused on the chair he'd barely looked at the magazines on the seat. "Yeah, sure. With any luck, I can get a few dollars for them."

Maybe more than that. He knew a few collectors who'd pay ten, twenty bucks a pop for some of the older magazines. But he wouldn't tell the old lady that. He'd offer her a fraction of what they were worth and make a nice profit.

And the chair...? He slid his hand across the delicate seat back and top rail. Howe Brothers chairs were hard to find, and the market for them was always hot. The last time a finely crafted piece like this had come up for bid, it had fetched nearly a quarter million.

"I'll take the magazines," he said. "I'll take those Depression glass pieces I saw in the cupboard. And this chair. I'll give you a hundred bucks for the lot."

The old girl's expression lit up. "My word. A hundred dollars. That'll come in handy. Since my husband passed on, I've been strapped for cash. And my health..." She smiled and the deep lines etched around her eyes crinkled. "Well, I'm not getting any younger. My daughter says—"

"Alright, I'll give you two hundred," Frank put in before she could start listing all her aches and pains. Or caught on to his game.

"Two hundred? I sure could use that kind of money."

She certainly could, if her house was any indication. A mansion on Woonsocket's South Main Street, at the edge of the city's historic district, this dump had seen better days. Her folks had probably been textile barons with a lot of dough at one time, before the mills shuttered and business relocated overseas.

But times were tough for everyone, especially him. If he could get that chair for a mere two bills, put it up for auction, and score a big payday, there'd be happy days ahead for old Frank. "I'll pay you cash if you want."

"But, Mr. Ford, I feel I should warn you. That chair is bad luck."

He began to toss the magazines into a box, barely listening. "You don't say?"

"Oh, yes. The chair's been in my family for over a hundred years. And it's been unlucky for just as long. Mama told a story of how Grandfather Hebert died after he tripped over the chair at the top of those stairs." She gestured to the staircase, covered with faded green carpeting and each step littered with junk. "Grandfather tumbled fanny-over-teakettle all the way to the bottom. Broke his neck."

"That's too bad." Frank tucked the magazine with Marilyn Monroe on the cover into the box with extra care. He could get a hundred, maybe more for this one.

Celina sighed tragically. "Mama said grandfather was mixed up in crooked land deals, and the law would've nabbed him sooner or later. So, I suppose justice was served in its fashion." She eyed the chair with a doubtful expression. "Are you *sure* you want it?"

"I'm sure. Look, I'll give you five hundred for everything. The magazines will pay for themselves. The chair's not so valuable, but I know some people who like this beat up old stuff."

"Heavens." She clasped an age-mottled hand to her breast. "Five hundred dollars for that unlucky old thing? Did I tell you my Uncle Wilbert had a heart attack and died, right here in this chair? He was cheating on his wife, the rascal, but still, such a shame for him to die so young."

Frank placed a Depression glass sugar bowl and creamer in the box with the magazines, eager to finish this deal and get out. He'd already jacked up his price well beyond what he wanted to pay, and if he let her keep yapping, he could get stuck here forever.

"Then there was my cousin Horatio." Celina pursed her lips. "He was a piece of work. Do you remember years ago when all that money was embezzled from City Bank? Oh, of course you don't, you're far too young. Well, Horatio stole the bank's money, but that thieving devil never faced the law. He was staying here for a few days and Mama found him dead on the floor one cold morning. Turns out he stood on the chair to change a light bulb and, well, something went wrong, and he somehow electrocuted himself."

Frank scoffed and Celina gazed at him, her eyes widening.

"It's the truth, Mr. Ford. Terrible things happen to people around this chair." She sighed. "It's nothing but bad luck."

Frank struggled not to roll his eyes. The old bat's superstition and ghost stories wouldn't scare him off. The chair would be good luck to him. He'd finally be able to pay Louise the back child support he owed her, and his kids wouldn't call him Daddy Deadbeat anymore. He could pay off his debts. That is if he actually paid up. He could take the cash he'd make from the chair and run. Stiff Louise and his creditors. Run away from Rhode Island's cold winters and go someplace warm. Someplace where the child support cops couldn't find him.

"Listen, Mrs. Chouinard. I understand your reluctance to part with something that's been in the family for so long, but you said it yourself, you need the money. What do you say I give you seven-fifty for all of this?"

"Wel-l-l-l..."

"You drive a hard bargain. I know I won't make my money back, but because it's the Christmas season, I'll give you one thousand and that's my final offer."

She glanced at the chair, then back at Frank. He gave her one of his *trust me* grins. The kind of smile that always suckered his creditors. And the ladies. Especially the old ladies.

She finally caved with a reluctant nod.

Frank smiled for real this time. He paid her in cash as promised, every last penny he had.

Frank steered his truck carefully out of the snow-slicked driveway of Celina Chouinard's home. He waited until he put the old lady's house well behind him before he glanced in satisfaction at the chair on the front seat next to him.

The chair barely fit in the cab, but no way would he store it in the back of the truck where he'd stashed the magazines and the Depression glass. He didn't care about those items, but he feared the chair might be damaged by the wintry mix of sleet and snow falling steadily in the night.

The storm had really kicked up in the last hour and the lazy-ass road crews had yet to get around to sanding or salting the slick pavement. Icy snow daggers cut across the dark road in front of him, making it hard to see.

Frank let his mind drift to someplace sunny and warm as he drove. With any luck, he could have the chair at auction by the beginning of the new year. With a little more luck, he'd be sipping a Mai-Tai on a tropical beach a month later. Far, far away from this cold mess.

A traffic light loomed ahead, barely visible in the storm. He didn't see the light blink from yellow to red until too late. A boat-sized Buick shot across the intersection. Frank jerked the steering wheel to avoid T-boning the vehicle. His truck fishtailed on the slippery road. He lost control and skidded directly toward an electrical utility box on the corner.

At the last second, he jammed both feet on the brakes. The box in the truck bed slammed into the cab wall behind him. Glass smashed. Momentum drove the chair forward and it spanked into the dashboard. Finally, his truck slid to a stop, inches from disaster. Frank leaned on the horn and swore a blue streak as the Buick's taillights disappeared into the night.

"Jerk," he muttered.

He punched on the overhead light and frantically checked the chair. No damage. No gashes or breaks. He sighed with relief. The Depression glass in the back was most likely a goner, the magazines an icy mess, but his chair was fine.

He laughed. What did that old broad say about bad luck?

Frank had a feeling his run of bad luck was over.

Celina Chouinard arrived at *Frank's Finds & Antiques* the next morning as soon as the roads were clear. She had to take a cab, which she didn't like, but her fingers had grown too stiff to grip the wheel of her ancient Lincoln, so she couldn't drive anymore. She felt the need to see Mr. Ford, and so she'd called Yellow Cab to get her there.

The driver helped her from the taxi, and she asked him to wait. She clutched her black patent-leather pocketbook to her wool coat as she inched forward along the crusty snow. The antique shop was housed on the first floor of a small, two-story brick building. A short flight of metal stairs led up to an apartment on the upper floor where Celina supposed Mr. Ford lived.

She spotted his truck, with the name of his shop painted on the door, parked out front—along with a couple of police cars and an ambulance.

Celina gaped at the scene at the bottom of the metal steps. Several policemen and paramedics gathered around Mr. Ford's stiff, snow-dusted body.

"Dear me." She tottered carefully forward and tugged on one of the cops' coat sleeves. "What happened, Officer?"

"He slipped on the top step, ma'am," the cop said, giving her a kind smile. "Cracked his head when he fell. He was dead in an instant."

"The poor man."

"At least it was quick. He was out here all night. No one noticed until the storm let up. Odd that he fell. There's no snow or ice up there. The porch overhang kept the landing bone dry. Guess it was just bad luck."

Celina looked up and saw her chair on the landing above, standing upright and sheltered in the enclosure of the small porch. *Bad luck, indeed.* She felt a pang of remorse, but only a small one. She'd tried to warn Mr. Ford. Several times. He wouldn't listen. Greedy men like him never listened.

"Officer, I came to pick up my chair. I was going to sell it to the dead man, but I changed my mind. Do you think I could just take it?"

He took off his hat and scratched his head, considering. Celina coughed a bit, made sure she teetered in a feeble way, and the young man gave in.

"Don't see why not. We don't need it for evidence. It's not like the chair killed him." The policeman chuckled. "I'll get it and bring it to your cab."

Back at home, the cab driver carried the chair inside. She told him to put it back in its spot in the hall then gave him a big tip. Why not? She had some extra money now. But the thousand dollars wouldn't last long.

Carrying a cup of hot tea, Celina headed into the den and sat down at her desk. She opened her laptop and typed, "antique dealers near me" into the browser.

As she sipped her tea, she searched for the name of a dealer with the most one-star reviews.

Thank you for reading *Clues & Chills*. I hope you enjoyed the stories as much as I did writing them. I'd appreciate it if you could help others find this collection by leaving a review.

And don't forget to visit my website for more information on me and all of my books. While you're there, please take a moment to sign up for my once-a-month newsletter, where you'll get updates on what I'm working on, plus exclusive content, free books, and all kinds of other goodies. Just stop by my website to join the fun! JanetRayeStevens.com

Now, as an extra bonus, here's a sneak peek of BERYL BLUE, TIME COP, the first book in my Beryl Blue series of adventures in time. Enjoy!

BERYL BLUE
TIME COP

"A perfect blend of historical fiction, a bit of sci-fi, and wonderful romance. A really fun read."

Hurled from 2015 to WWII, feisty librarian Beryl Blue is tasked with stopping a time traveling assassin from killing a soldier on leave and changing history forever. The bad guy is one problem, his target is another. Beryl's stunned to find herself falling for gruff and stubborn Army sergeant Tom 'Sully' Sullivan, who makes it abundantly clear he can take care of himself.

With an assassin on their heels and all of history on her shoulders, Beryl scrambles to protect a man who refuses to be protected—and keep her heart intact.

"BERYL BLUE, TIME COP," I shouted. "Stop!"

The guy I chased didn't. Didn't even slow down. Which put me in A Mood, as Grandma Blue had called my teenaged temperament. But who could blame me for getting annoyed? My ankle still bitched from last week's not-so-fun run in 1599, chasing that guy stalking Shakespeare. The trip through the temporal gate today had been its usual shake-and-bake fun. Now here I was in 1977, running after an overdue time tourist on a steamy hot July afternoon.

While wearing a policewoman's uniform with a worsted wool jacket and skirt.

And pantyhose.

What's more, the time-perp I pursued zipped along on roller skates. Sprinting after him made my ankle throb like the dickens.

"Come on, man," I called. "Stop!"

The guy pumped his chalky legs harder, picking up speed. His skate wheels rumbled as he zigzagged around pedestrians. He was cruising for a close encounter with my cack .28, and I was going to oblige. Time Scope Excursions had a whole list of rules for time tourists, but number one was to come home when your vacation in the past had ended. No exceptions.

That's where I came in. My job was to find and extract overdue time tourists any way necessary.

I slipped the weapon out of its holster and armed it. My quarry skated into the clear. I aimed. The guy fell. Not from the cack's invisible burst of scorching juice. From a crack. In the sidewalk. Flew ass over teakettle and landed flat on his squishy butt. To my relief, and to the delight of Hampton Beach's feathery-hairdo crowd, who cheered his triple-gainer wipeout.

I holstered the cack and limped over to him. He grimaced up at me. Would've been comical if he didn't look so pathetic, splayed like a starfish in his disco roller boogie outfit, his short shorts riding up high enough for all 1977 to get a good look at his package.

I averted my eyes. I'm dainty that way.

"You wouldn't have caught me if I didn't trip," he said, sitting up and wincing in pain.

"Seriously? I would've killed you." I tapped my holster for emphasis. Time Scope didn't fool around. Better to take out a rogue time tourist than have them upset the timeline by running wild in the past.

I helped the guy to stand. He wobbled like a newborn colt until he got his balance.

"Please, ma'am, don't bring me back," he said. Begged, really.

"Ma'am?" Yikes. I was twenty-four, still got carded everywhere I went. This guy was pushing forty. "Do I look like your grandmother?"

"I'm sorry, ma'am, uh, officer. But, please, don't take me back. I don't *belong* in 2130."

Oh, crap. He was one of *them*. A runner. He hadn't stepped through one of Time Scope's temporal gates to go on an expensive vacation, or even with a nefarious plan to loot the treasures of the past. He'd intended his time trip to be only one way. He'd intended to disappear into history.

"That's what they all say," I muttered, avoiding his pleading eyes, because—irony alert—I didn't belong in 2130 either. Six months ago, I was a happy wannabe librarian living my life in the early 21st century. Well, sort of happy. Okay, pretty miserable if truth be told. But the thing was, I could never, ever go back to that time. "And, seriously, 1977? I mean, *Star Wars* comes out, I get that. But of all the time periods in all of history, why run here? Why now?"

"I love the music. And..." He sniffed the air. "You smell that? What is it? It's heavenly."

I'd caught the smell too, had packed on five pounds just from the aroma. "Fried dough."

His milky blue eyes lit up. "Fried dough," he said with reverence, then his voice cracked with sudden panic. "Please don't take me back. Say you killed me. Say anything. *Please* let me stay."

This guy hit new levels of pathetic, going straight for my heart. Guess he didn't get the memo. I used to let emotions guide me. Not anymore. Glo Reid, Time Scope and a lying guy named Jake Tyson had seen to that. Now I was nothing but a cold-hearted company goon.

At least, that's what I kept telling myself.

"Look, disco man," I said, harsher than I intended. I would *not* let this pathetic puppy get to me. "You *can't* stay. A skate down the sidewalk in 1977 won't change anything, but if you disappear into the past? The future. Is. Screwed. So, no way I'm leaving you here, *capiche?*"

My bad ass act seemed to scare him more than threatening him with the weapon. He came along quietly when I suggested we find a spot where we could disappear without witnesses. I towed him away from the beach toward the bustling downtown, looking for an alley. He gazed wistfully at the boat-sized cars clogging the street, the people dressed in colors that would make Joseph's *Technicolor Dreamcoat* look subdued, and the stores advertising wares still made in the USA.

"Wait." I stopped, spotting a sale sign in a store window. I felt a smile coming on. I hadn't smiled in a while. It felt good. "A quick stop, then back home and off to the cage with you."

"That's contraband," my prisoner cried when he saw where we were headed. "I'll tell unless you let me go."

"No, you won't." I patted my holster again and he shut up. But to be on the safe side, I decided to invest in a big piece of fried dough for his enjoyment before we went back to the future.

———

"You bucking for Time Cop of the year, Beryl?" Carmine slapped the buzzer and the holding cage door clanged sideways. "That's the third temporal ex-pat you brung in this month."

I shrugged. "It's an epidemic."

Carmine scratched his salt-and-pepper mustache then dug into his ear for good measure. "I don't get why anyone would run to an earlier time. We got everything you could ever want here."

"I know, right?" I adjusted the package in the brown paper bag tucked under my arm. Not *every*thing.

I signaled to my disco friend to wipe fried dough crumbs off his face then pushed him into the cell. He rolled across the tile, and I held my breath as he tripped-fell onto a bench. The guy had been through enough without the added indignity of face planting in front of Time Scope's second shift. The cell door slid shut and I turned away from his sad blue eyes.

Poor guy. He'd be off to rehab in the morning. Not the kind of rehab anyone from my 21st century home would recognize. No twelve steps, no daily affirmations. It was a quick fix that involved some kind of laser lobotomy. The guy would be all happy-happy, joy-joy and would never want to roller boogie in another time period again.

I pushed the guy's brain-scrambling fate out of my mind. What he'd done was dangerous. I cringed to think what could've happened to the historical timeline if I hadn't caught him.

After what seemed like weeks of paperwork, I returned my 1970s cop uniform to wardrobe and changed into jeans and a windbreaker. I tucked my contraband into my backpack and took a Metro-Slide home in the fading daylight of an April afternoon.

The lights in my high-rise studio apartment popped on as I entered. Jenjen, my monstrous Maine coon cat, met me at the door. I took off my jacket and hefted my backpack onto the kitchen counter, pushing aside a stack of books. Jenjen leapt up with impressive agility for such a fat cat and stuck his face into the backpack as I unzipped it.

"That's not for you." I pushed him away and pulled out a six-pack of Budweiser.

I'd broken one of Time Scope's many rules—no souvenirs. But it wasn't like the powers that signed my paycheck dared to squawk. After everything I'd gone through on the company's behalf, they owed me. Big time.

I slipped my finger through the ring-tab on one of the beer cans and popped the top. The beer was foamy from the time trip, but still cold.

"Can't get beer like this here in 2130," I said, taking a sip and scratching behind Jenjen's ear. "Not without a prescription, anyway."

He twitched his tail, a signal in any century that said, "Not interested. Feed me."

A bowl of kitty chow later, he washed his paws contentedly as I settled into my chair and started on my own dinner, the second can of my contraband six pack.

"Entertainment Communications Interface," I said, resting my sore ankle on a footstool. A portion of my apartment's west wall dissolved at my command to reveal a giant TV screen. Several function icons popped up. "Music." The icons faded, except for the G-clef, which blossomed in size. "World War Two mix. Random."

The aching, melancholy "I'll Be Seeing You," sung by Rosemary Clooney, softly filled the air. My heart wrenched as the memories rushed in like a flood tide. I thought of the roller boogie disco man and the music he loved. Music that made him give up everything to flee to another time. I didn't get his passion for the thumping '70s disco beat, but I got where the passion came from. I'd risk everything, too, if I could go back to that one moment, forget about the timeline, and just go.

Go to *him*.

Before I could stop myself, I had the photograph in my hand. I'd never uploaded it to the Interface. I didn't want anyone else to get access to it, whether by accident or design. I wanted it where only I could see it, only I could hold it. I'd tucked the photo into a drawer in my bedside table, promising myself I'd only look at it once a month.

Yesterday. I made that promise yesterday.

"What can I say, Sully?" I murmured, gazing at the photo. "I'm weak."

There they were, in glorious four-by-five black-and-white. Four GIs crowded around a small table littered with beer bottles and shot glasses, looking like the cast of a John Wayne World War II movie. Marco, Griff, Stan...

And Sully.

I slid my thumb over Sully's face. I longed to stroke that impossibly strong jaw for real. To touch that Grand Canyon-deep chin cleft. Run my fingers through his thick, copper-red hair. A cigarette dangled from his lips, as usual. Smoke coiled around his eyes, making him squint. He was smiling. The one honest, happy moment before he shipped out. Before places like Normandy and Bastogne. Before the terrible events that tore us apart forever.

I was in the picture, perched on Sully's lap. I looked pretty. I was smiling too. Really smiling. I was so soft then. Not my body. I'd always been a solid size fourteen. My heart was soft. Sully had his arm around my waist, his free hand rested on my leg. I could almost feel his touch, his hand on my thigh, his fingers gently massaging. The ache in my heart doubled.

I had to stop doing this, had to stop pining for a memory and longing for a man I could never be with. A man I'd lost long ago.

I reached for another can and popped the top on my third beer, hoping the buzz beginning to cloud my brain would help me forget.

Forget, for just a little while.

How did a librarian from 2015 end up as a time cop in the twenty second century? Find out in the first book of Beryl's adventures through time, *Beryl Blue, Time Cop*

Author Janet Raye Stevens fell in love with the mystery, history, and time travel genres as a kid and has been hopping around through the centuries solving crimes in her fiction ever since.

A Derringer and Silver Falchion Award finalist and winner of the Daphne du Maurier award for the WWII-set A MOMENT AFTER DARK, Janet writes historical and contemporary mysteries, time travel adventures, and the occasional Christmas romance with humor, heart, and a dash of suspense.

She lives with her family in New England.